Before he could ask what was wrong, or why she was here, she was in his arms and kissing him.

At that point all Deacon could do was react. And in that moment, with the woman he had once loved in his arms again after all this time, he couldn't push her away.

Her mouth was hot and demanding as she kissed him. This was nothing like the sweet, hesitant kisses of their teenage years. Cecelia was now a grown woman who knew exactly what she wanted and how to get it. And from the looks of it, she wanted Deacon.

He tried not to think about how her fiancé could've been the one to teach her these new tricks.

That was the thought that yanked Deacon away from Cecelia's kiss. He took a step back, bracing her shoulders and holding her away from him. "What are you doing here, Cecelia?" he asked. "Shouldn't you be making out with your rich fiancé right now instead of me?"

Cecelia silently held up her hand, wiggling the bare finger that had previously held the gigantic diamond he'd noticed that afternoon at the presentation. So the engagement was off, and just since he'd seen her last.

* * *

Expecting the Billionaire's Baby is part of the series Texas Cattleman's Club: Blackmail—No secret—or heart—is safe in Royal, Texas...

Dear Reader,

As I neared over twenty titles with Desire, I noticed something: I hadn't been asked to participate in the Texas Cattleman's Club series. Now, I get it, cowboys aren't really my strength, but I have to admit my feelings were hurt just a teensy bit. So like any professional, I whined about it on Twitter to my editors. They hadn't realized I wanted to do one! Of course I did. So when the next series came around, they found the perfect plot for me.

There's not a cowboy in sight. But that's okay, because instead we have Deacon Chase, the sexy hotelier from the wrong side of Royal. He never fit in with the rich rancher's kids and Dallas elite, but that didn't keep him from catching—and keeping—Cecelia Morgan's eye back in high school. Years later, he's returning to Royal a billionaire with something to prove to the town and the girl that broke his heart all those years ago!

I can't wait for you to read Deacon and Cecelia's story. If you enjoy it, tell me by visiting my website at www.andrealaurence.com, like my fan page on Facebook or follow me on Twitter. I love to hear from my readers!

Enjoy!

Andrea

ANDREA LAURENCE

EXPECTING THE
BILLIONAIRE'S BABY

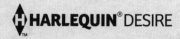

Special thanks and acknowledgment are given to Andrea Laurence for her contribution to the Texas Cattleman's Club: Blackmail miniseries.

Recycling programs for this product may not exist in your area.

ISBN-13: 978-0-373-83837-0

Expecting the Billionaire's Baby

Copyright © 2017 by Harlequin Books S.A.

HARLEQUIN®
www.Harlequin.com

Printed in U.S.A.

Andrea Laurence is an award-winning author of contemporary romances filled with seduction and sass. She has been a lover of reading and writing stories since she was young. A dedicated West Coast girl transplanted into the Deep South, she is thrilled to share her special blend of sensuality and dry, sarcastic humor with readers.

Books by Andrea Laurence

Harlequin Desire

Brides and Belles

Snowed In with Her Ex
Thirty Days to Win His Wife
One Week with the Best Man
A White Wedding Christmas

Secrets of Eden

Undeniable Demands
A Beauty Uncovered
Heir to Scandal
Her Secret Husband

Millionaires of Manhattan

What Lies Beneath
More Than He Expected
His Lover's Little Secret
The CEO's Unexpected Child

Hawaiian Nights

The Pregnancy Proposition
The Baby Proposal

Texas Cattleman's Club: Blackmail

Expecting the Billionaire's Baby

Visit her Author Profile page at Harlequin.com, or andrealaurence.com, for more titles.

To My Fellow TCC Authors—

I loved sharing a little blackmail between friends.
Looking forward to working with you all again!

And To Our Super Editor Charles—

If you can keep up with all twelve stories,
you're officially a superhero.
I'm going to buy you a cape.
Maybe some tights.

One

"You can do this, Cecelia."

Cecelia Morgan attempted to encourage herself as she looked over her portfolio for the hundredth time. Tomorrow, she was presenting her design plans to the board of directors of the new Bellamy Hotel. This was a big step for her and her company, To the Moon. The company she started after college specialized in children's furniture, bedding and toys. From the beginning she had targeted a high-end market, catering to wealthy parents who were looking for luxury products for their children.

The company had been a success from the very

start. What had begun as a small online boutique had exploded into a series of stores across the United States after a celebrity posted on social media about how much they loved one of TTM's nursery designs. Cecelia had been forced to open her own production facility and warehouse outside her hometown of Royal, Texas, to keep up with the demand.

The portfolio on the desk in front of her, however, could take To the Moon to the next level. Designing furniture, toys and accessories for pampered little ones had been her first love, but now Cecelia was ready for her business to mature along with her tastes. The Bellamy Hotel was her chance to make this a reality.

The Bellamy was a brand-new five-star resort opening right outside Royal. Owner Shane Delgado had contacted Cecelia about decorating and furnishing the hotel about a month ago, after a previous designer had been fired well into the process. This would be a big step for Cecelia. If she could secure the contract with The Bellamy, it would give her the footing she needed to branch out into the luxury adult furniture market.

As her daddy always said, if you're not moving forward, you might as well be moving backward. She was successful, but that wasn't enough for the

Morgans. Her subsidiary of To the Moon—Luna Fine Furnishings—could change everything for her.

She was shocked that Shane had reached out to her, given he was pretty clear he'd dismissed her as part of the mean girls clique, along with her best friends Simone and Naomi. Admittedly, she wasn't very nice to his girlfriend Brandee and recent gossip had been less than flattering about Cecelia and her friends. Some even suspected them of being behind the recent blackmailings. Shane was taking a huge leap of faith inviting her to submit her ideas for this incredible opportunity; she wasn't about to screw this up.

Cecelia gathered up everything into her portfolio binder and slipped it into her leather briefcase. She'd probably gone over it a hundred times already. She needed to stop fiddling with it and just let it lie. It was perfect. Some of her best work yet. As usual, she was putting too much pressure on herself. Her parents certainly didn't help matters. They always held Cecelia, their only child, to very high standards and never accepted anything less than perfection.

She supposed that was why she was so successful. Brent and Tilly Morgan were practically Texas royalty and had raised their daughter to follow in their footsteps. She went to the best private schools, rode horses and competed in dressage in high school, and went on to graduate summa cum laude with a business degree from a prestigious Ivy League university. Anything less for the younger Morgan would've been unacceptable.

While her parents had been supportive both emotionally and financially when it came to her company, Cecelia always worried that their support came at a price. If Luna Fine Furnishings wasn't the success that she hoped for, she might never hear the end of it. The last thing she needed was for her father to pat her on the back and tell her that maybe she needed to just stick with the baby things. You know…woman stuff. Or worse yet, to hand the business over to someone else and focus on settling down with Chip Ashford to make actual babies instead of baby furniture.

She wasn't opposed to settling down with Chip— he was her fiancé after all—but she certainly didn't want to throw away everything that she'd worked for in the process. Chip was a Texas senator, and he had been very supportive of her business so far. But Cecelia got the feeling that once they got married, Chip might feel the same way as her parents did.

It wasn't that she didn't want kids. Cecelia wanted her own children more than anything. But she was confident that she could be both a mother and the CEO of her own company. She didn't intend to set one ambition aside for the other.

A chime sounded on Cecelia's phone. She reached for it and tapped the screen to open up the Snapchat notification she'd just received for a private message. It took her a moment to realize what she was actually looking at. The picture was of a document with small text, but the header at the top brought a sinking feeling to her stomach. It read "Certificate of Birth" with the seal of the state of Texas on the bottom corner. The message across the screen was far more worrisome.

Somebody has got a secret.

Cecelia looked once more at the photo before it disappeared. It was then that she realized that this wasn't just any birth certificate, it was *her* original birth certificate. The one issued before she was adopted by the Morgans.

For a moment, Cecelia almost couldn't breathe. Her adoption had always been kept a secret. Everyone, including members of her extended family, believed that Cecelia was Brent and Tilly's biological daughter. Even Cecelia had believed it until her thirteenth birthday. That night, they'd told her that she was adopted but that they had kept it a secret for her own protection. The unfortunate truth was that her birth mother had been a junkie, and child services had taken Cecelia away from her when she was only a few weeks old. Her mother had overdosed not long after that, and she was put up for adoption. The Morgans thought that it was best if Cecelia's birth mother and that dark past were kept secret.

But someone had found out.

Cecelia didn't know how—she hadn't even seen her original birth certificate before. A new one had been issued when her adoption was finalized, so someone had done some serious sleuthing to find it.

Another image popped up on her screen. This one was a message written in letters cut from magazines like some sort of ransom note. She supposed that in some way, it *was* a ransom note. It demanded that twenty-five thousand dollars be wired to an account within twenty-four hours or her secret would be exposed to the entire town. It was signed, Maverick.

Considering everything that had been happening in Royal, Texas, lately, she should've known she would be targeted eventually. Maverick had been wreaking havoc on the lives of Royal residents for the past few months. This anonymous blackmailer had been the talk of the town, and everyone at the Texas Cattleman's Club had suspicions about who it could be. The most recent suspects had been Cecelia herself, along with Naomi and Simone.

Cecelia was a busy woman. She ran her own business, served as arm candy for her fiancé's various political events, was busy keeping up appearances for her parents and for Chip... She hardly had time in her schedule to get a manicure, much less to research and dig up dirt on her fellow residents. Her busy schedule and high standards made her come off as a bit snobbish, and Cecelia supposed she was, but she was no blackmailer. Unfortunately, the only way to prove it was to let everyone know that she was Maverick's latest victim.

That certainly wasn't an option. She couldn't have the whole town knowing that her entire life was a lie.

Unfortunately, this wasn't just her secret. Her parents had built their lives around their perfect "biological" daughter. They'd lied to countless family members and friends to keep up the charade, but they'd only done it to protect her. Paying Maverick was probably the only way to shield Brent and Tilly from the fallout.

But hers wasn't the only family she had to worry about. The Ashfords would have a fit. Chip came from a certain kind of family, and he believed that Cecelia was cut from the same cloth. Would Chip call off the engagement if he found out the truth? Their relationship was more about appearances and family alliances than love, but she hoped that Chip cared enough about her not to throw everything away if her secret got out. As far as she was concerned, she was a Morgan, through and through.

And as a Morgan, it was her responsibility to safeguard her and her family's reputation, or tomorrow's presentation would go down in flames. Her reputation where Shane was concerned was hanging on by a thread as it was. Surely, he wouldn't want a scandal to interfere with his hotel's grand opening.

But when did it stop? Would Maverick be content with the first payment, or would he drag this out until Cecelia was broke and her business was bankrupted?

Cecelia clutched her head in her hands and fought off a pending migraine. She'd suddenly found herself stuck between a rock and a hard place, and there was no easy way out of this. She either paid Maverick, or the truth of her adoption would be spread all over town. The clock was ticking.

She wasn't sure what her path forward would be, but Cecelia knew what she was doing next. In her life whenever a crisis arose, Cecelia always called her daddy. This conversation, however, was one that needed to be had in person. She didn't know how Maverick had found out about her adoption, but if her phone lines were tapped or her computer was being monitored, she couldn't risk anything but face-to-face communication.

It took Cecelia over an hour for her to reach her parents' mansion outside Houston. It was nearly ten o'clock by the time she arrived, but her parents would still be awake. As expected, she found her father sitting in his library. He was reading a book and smoking one of his favorite cigars.

Brent Morgan looked up in surprise when he noticed his daughter standing in the doorway of his library. "What are you doing here, sweetheart? Your mother didn't tell me were stopping by tonight."

Cecelia took a few steps into her father's favorite room and took a seat in the leather chair across from him. "She doesn't know I'm here. I'm in trouble, Daddy."

Furrowing his brow, he set aside his book and stubbed out his cigar. "What is it? Are you and Chip having problems?"

"No, this isn't about Chip." With a sigh, Cecelia told her father about the message she had received. His expression had morphed from concerned, to angry, to anxious as she spoke. "I've got twenty-four hours to wire them twenty-five thousand dollars, or everyone is going to know the truth."

"Our family can't afford a scandal like this. And imagine the pain this would bring to the Ashfords. Surely this isn't what you want. You're just going to have to pay him," he said, matter-of-factly.

Cecelia hated being put in a position where she had no options, and being under Maverick's thumb was the last place she wanted to be. The only real way to combat blackmail was by exposing the truth before the attacker could. If they beat Maverick to the punch they could put their own spin on her adoption and why they'd lied about it.

"Are you sure, Daddy? I mean, I know you and Mother were trying to protect me, but I'm a grown woman now. I'd rather the story not get out. However, would it be the end of the world if people discovered I was adopted? Does it change anything, really?"

"It absolutely does!" her father said with his face flushing red, making his salt-and-pepper hair appear more starkly white against his skin. "We've lied to everyone we know for thirty years. This would ruin our reputation. And what would the Ashfords think? They wouldn't understand. Neither would my customers or my friends. I could lose business. Hell, you could get thrown out of the Texas Cattleman's Club. It's social suicide, and your mother's heart couldn't take the scandal. No," he insisted. "This stays a secret. Period. I will loan you the money if you need it to pay the blackmailer, but you *will* pay him."

Cecelia noted the finality in her father's tone. It had been the same when she was an unruly child, the same when she was a teenager testing her boundaries. She was an adult now, but Brent Morgan was still in charge. She didn't have the nerve to go against him then, and she certainly didn't have the nerve to do it now. She'd come here for his advice, and she'd be a fool not to take it.

"No, I have the money. I'll make the transfer in the morning. I just hope it is enough to put an end to all of this."

"It has to be," her father said. "I refuse to have our family turned into laughingstocks."

Cecelia sighed in resignation and got up from her seat. "I'll take care of it, Daddy."

Deacon Chase turned his restored 1965 Corvette Stingray down the main street of Royal, Texas. It'd been thirteen years since he'd looked at this town in his rearview mirror and swore he'd never set foot in this narrow-minded, Texas dust trap again. The whole flight over from France, he questioned why he was coming back. Yes, it was good business, and working with his old friend from high school, Shane Delgado, had always been a pleasant experience. But when Shane mentioned that he wanted to build a resort in their hometown of Royal, he should have passed.

Then again, when else would he get the chance to show the town and the people who rejected him that he was better than them? Sure, back then he'd just been a poor kid with few prospects. He was the son of a grocery store clerk and the local car mechanic. He'd gotten to go to private school with all the rich kids only because his parents had been adamant that Deacon make something of himself, and they'd put every dime they had toward his schooling. Even then he had worked in the cafeteria to bridge the gap in tuition. Nobody else had expected much out of him, and those were the people who even acknowledged he existed. As far as most the residents of Royal were concerned, Deacon had never fit in, never would fit in and needed to accept his station in life.

No one had expected him to take his hobby of restoring cars and parlay the skills and money into restoring houses. They certainly hadn't expected him to take the profit from those houses and put it into renovating hotels. Now the kid who worked in the cafeteria was a billionaire and the owner of the most glamorous resort in Cannes, France, the Hotel de Rêve, among others.

The only person in Royal who had ever believed in him was Cecelia. Back in high school, she'd pushed him to be the best person he could be. Considering that she'd held herself to such high standards, he'd been flattered that she saw so much potential in him when most of the people in high school either ignored him or taunted him. Cecelia had said he was a diamond in the rough. *Her* diamond in the rough.

It'd certainly blown the minds of all the boys at school that Cecelia had chosen Deacon instead of one of them. What could he offer her after all? A free carton of milk with her lunch? It turned out that he'd had plenty to offer her. He could still remember how many hours they'd spent lying in the back of his pickup truck talking. Kissing. Dreaming aloud about their future together. Deacon and Cecelia had had big plans for their lives after graduation.

Step one had been to get the hell out of Royal, Texas. Step two had been to live happily-ever-after.

As Deacon came to a stop at the traffic light at the intersection of Main Street and First Avenue, he shook his head in disgust. He had been a fool to think any of that would ever happen. He might have fancy hotels and expensive suits, sports cars and a forty-foot yacht docked in the French Riviera, but Deacon knew, and everybody else knew, that Cecelia was too good for him.

It hadn't taken long for Cecelia to figure that out, too.

The light turned green, and Deacon continued down the road to where his father's old garage used to be. When he'd made his first million, Deacon had moved his parents out of Royal and into a nice subdivision in central Florida. There, they could enjoy their early retirement without the meddling of the snooty residents of Royal. His father had sold the shop, and now a new shopping center was sitting where it used to be. A lot had changed in the last thirteen years.

Deacon couldn't help but wonder how much Cecelia had changed. He tried not to cyberstalk her, but from time to time he couldn't help looking over the Houston society pages to see what she was up to. The grainy black-and-white pictures hardly did her beauty justice, he was certain. The last time he'd seen her, she'd been a young woman, barely eighteen. Even then, Deacon had been certain that she was the most beautiful woman he would ever see in person. He would bet that time had been kind to his Cecelia.

Not that it mattered. The most recent article he'd stumbled across in the paper had included the announcement of her engagement to Chip Ashford. He remembered Chip from high school. He was a rich, entitled, first-class douche bag. Deacon was fairly certain that that hadn't changed, but if Cecelia was willing to marry him, she certainly wasn't the girl that he remembered. Back then, she'd hardly given Chip the time of day.

Mr. and Mrs. Morgan must be so proud of her now. She'd finally made a respectable choice in a man.

Turning off the main drag, Deacon headed down the narrow country road out of Royal that led to his latest real estate acquisition. The rustic yet luxurious lodge that was to serve as his home base in the area stood on three acres of wooded land several miles outside town. He'd bought the property sight unseen when he decided to take on The Bellamy project with Shane. He couldn't be happier with the place. It was very much his style, although it was a far cry from the elegant European architecture and design that he'd become accustomed to.

He hadn't really needed to buy the home. Deacon had no real intention of staying in Royal any longer than he had to. But the businessman in him had a hard time passing up a good deal, and it seemed a shame to throw money away on renting a place while they built the hotel. He had no regrets. It was his happy retreat, away from the society jungles of Royal.

When he pulled up in front of the lodge, he was surprised to find Shane Delgado's truck parked out front. Deacon parked the Corvette in his garage, then stepped out front to meet his friend and business partner.

Deacon hadn't had many friends back in school. Basically none. But his side business of buying and restoring cars had drawn Shane's attention. Shane had actually bought Deacon's very first restoration, a 1975 cherry-red Ford pickup truck with white leather seats. Deacon had been damn proud of that truck, especially when Shane had handed over the cash for it without questioning his asking price. They'd bonded then over a mutual love of cars and had continued to keep in touch over the years. When they both ended up in the real estate development business, it was natural for them to consider working together on a few projects.

"What's wrong now?" Deacon asked as he joined Shane at the bottom of his front steps.

While the construction of The Bellamy had gone relatively smoothly, Deacon was the silent partner. Shane bothered him with details only when something had gone awry. He joked with Shane once that he was getting to the point that he dreaded the sight of his friend's face.

"For once," Shane said with a smile, "I'm just here to hang out and have a drink with my friend. Everything at the hotel is going splendidly. Tomorrow, Cecelia Morgan will be presenting her designs to the board, based on your recommendation. Assuming we like what Cecelia did, and I hope I'm not going too far out on a limb here, we'll be moving forward and getting that much closer to opening the hotel."

Deacon slapped his friend on the back of the shoulder. "I wouldn't have brought her on board if I didn't think she was the best designer for the job. Come on in," he said as they started up the massive stone stairs to the front door. "Have you eaten?" he asked as they made their way into his office for a drink.

Shane nodded. "I have. Brandee is constantly feeding me. By the end of the year, I'm going to weigh three hundred pounds."

"You're a lucky man," Deacon said as he poured them both a couple of fingers of whiskey over ice. Shane had recently gotten involved with Brandee Lawless, the owner of the nearby Hope Springs Ranch. She was a tiny blonde spitfire, and one hell of a cook. "I'd be happy to have Brandee feeding me every night."

"I bet you would," Shane said. "But you need to just stick with your cultured European women."

Deacon chuckled at his friend's remark. He had certainly taken advantage of the local delicacies while he was in Europe. Even though it'd been years since he and Cecelia had broken up, it had soothed his injured pride to have a line of beautiful and exotic women waiting for their chance to be with him. He would never admit to anyone, especially Shane, that not a one of them held a candle to Cecelia in his mind.

Deacon and Shane sat there together, sipping their drinks and enjoying each other's company. They didn't get a lot of opportunities to just hang out anymore. Deacon's office, however, just begged for gentlemen to spend time in comfortable chairs and shoot the shit. The walls were lined with shelves containing leather-bound books that, frankly, came with the house and Deacon would never read. They did create a nice atmosphere, though, along with the oil paintings of landscapes and cattle that hung there. It was all very masculine Texas style.

"Can I ask you something?" Shane asked.

"Sure. What?"

"You do know that Cecelia's business specializes in children's furniture, right?"

Deacon tensed in his chair. Perhaps his office made Shane too comfortable, since he felt like prying into Deacon's motivations for wanting Cecelia for the job. "Yeah, I know. I also know that she's managed to turn her small company into a furniture and accessories juggernaut since she started it. She's always had a good eye for design."

"She does, I won't argue that. But hiring her to decorate The Bellamy is a huge risk. She and Brandee aren't exactly fans of each other. And what if she and her friends are actually behind the cyberattacks? That's not the kind of publicity we'd want for our hotel. I don't have to remind you how much we stand to lose if our gamble doesn't pay off."

"That's why we just asked her to submit a proposal along with the two other design firms. We haven't hired anybody yet. If she's out of her depth in this, or acts suspicious in any way, we thank her for her time and send her on her way. It's not ideal, but not the end of the world, either."

Shane narrowed his gaze at him. He obviously suspected that Deacon had ulterior motives in wanting Cecelia involved in the project. Deacon understood. He wasn't entirely sure that he didn't.

"I'm not sold on either of the other firm's designs. She's last to present, so if she flops tomorrow, it's going to set the project back weeks while we find yet another designer and they start from scratch. We have hotel bookings starting day one. Every delay costs us money."

Deacon just nodded. He was well aware that he was taking a risk. But for some reason, he had to do it. Perhaps he was a glutton for punishment. Perhaps he was looking for any excuse to see her again. He wasn't sure. The only thing he was sure of was that everything would turn out fine. "Relax, Shane. The project will finish on time and on budget with the amazing decor you're hoping for."

"And how do you know that?" Shane asked, sounding unconvinced.

"Because," Deacon said confidently, "Cecelia hasn't failed at anything in her entire life. She's not going to start now."

Two

"Welcome, Miss Morgan. Please have a seat."

Cecelia took two steps into the boardroom and stopped short as she recognized the man's voice. She looked up and found herself staring into the green-and-gold eyes of her past. She couldn't take a single step farther. Her heart stuttered as her mind raced to make sense of what she was seeing. It wasn't possible that Deacon Chase, her first love, was sitting at the head of the boardroom table beside Shane Delgado.

Deacon had disappeared from Royal almost immediately after they graduated from high school.

No one in town had seen or heard a word from him since then. She remembered being told that his parents had moved to Florida, and she had occasionally wondered what he had made of himself, but she hadn't had the heart to look him up and find out. She knew that it was best to keep Deacon a part of her past, and yet here he was, a critical element to the success of her future.

Cecelia realized she was standing awkwardly at the entrance to the conference room with the entire board of directors staring at her. She snapped out of it, pasting a wide smile on her face and walking to the front of the room where an empty seat was waiting for her. Beside him.

"Thank you, everyone, for having me here today. I'm very pleased to have the opportunity to present my designs for The Bellamy Hotel to the board. I'm really in love with what I have put together for you all today, and I hope it meets your expectations."

Deacon's cold gaze followed her around the room to where she had taken her seat, but she tried not to let it get to her. The man had every reason to hate her, so she shouldn't expect anything less.

She knew that Shane had a silent partner in The Bellamy project, but she'd never dreamed that it would be Deacon. She had a hard time believing it was even Deacon sitting there, considering how much he'd changed since she saw him last.

His lanky teenaged body had grown into it-self, with broad shoulders and muscular arms that strained against the fabric of his expensively tai-lored navy suit. His jaw was more square and hard-ened now, as though he was trying to hold in the venomous words he had for her. The lines etched around his eyes and into his furrowed brow made it look like he didn't smile much anymore.

That made Cecelia sad. The Deacon she remem-bered had been full of life, despite the miserable hand that he had been dealt as a child. Back in high school, he'd had so much potential in him, Cecelia just couldn't wait to see what he was going to do with his future.

Now she knew. It appeared as though Deacon had done extremely well for himself. He had gone from the kid working in the cafeteria to the man who held her future in his hands.

Opening her portfolio, she sorted through her pa-pers and prepared to give the presentation she had practiced repeatedly since Shane had called and of-fered her a chance to bid on the job. She pulled out several watercolor renderings of the designs, plac-ing them on the easel behind her. Then, taking a deep breath and looking at everyone but Deacon, Cecelia began her presentation.

It was easy for her to get lost in the details of her plan for the hotel. Discussing fabric choices, wooden furnishing pieces, style and design was what she knew best. She had a very distinct point of view that she wanted to express for The Bellamy to separate it from all the other high-class resorts in the Houston area.

Judging by the smiles and nods of the people sitting around the conference room table, she had hit it out of the park. The only person who looked less than impressed, of course, was Deacon. His eyes still focused on her like lasers, but his expression was unreadable.

"Does anyone have any questions?" She looked around the room, ready to field any of the board's concerns. No one spoke up.

Shane finally stood up and walked around the table to shake Cecelia's hand. "Thank you so much, Cecelia," he said with an oddly relieved smile on his face. "I admit I was reluctant to believe you were the right designer for the job, but I must say I'm very impressed. You've done a great job. You're the last to present your designs, so we will have to discuss your proposal, and then we will get back to you about contracts. If we decide to go with Luna Fine Furnishings, how long do you think it will be before you can start work on the hotel?"

Her heart was pounding, but whether it was from Shane's question or Deacon being mere inches away, she couldn't say. "I have already started putting the major furniture pieces into production at my manufacturing facility," Cecelia said. Several of the designs were tweaks of her existing furniture, and it was easy to get them started. "I also put in an order for the fabric, and it should arrive tomorrow. I took the risk, hoping that you would accept my proposal. If you don't like what I've done, I'm going to have to find a new home for about two hundred and fifty dressers."

The people around the table chuckled. Shane just smiled. "A risk-taker. I like it. Well, hopefully we will find a good home for all those dressers. We hope to open the resort by the end of the month. Do you think you can make that happen?"

By the end of the month? Cecelia's stomach started to ache with dread. Even with construction complete, that was an extremely tight schedule. Two hundred and fifty suites in a month! Although she was expecting the fabric for the curtains and upholstered chairs, it would still take time to make the pieces. She wasn't about to say no, however. She could sleep when April was over. "Absolutely. We may have to have our craftsmen working around the clock to get all the pieces together and the wallpaper on the walls, but I think we can make it happen."

Cecelia tried to keep her focus on Shane, but Deacon's appraising gaze kept drawing her attention away. He still wasn't smiling like everyone else. But he wasn't glaring at her angrily anymore, either. Now he was just watching. Thinking, processing. She had no idea what was going on inside Deacon's brain because he hadn't spoken since he welcomed her into the room. Part of her wished she knew. Part of her didn't.

"That all sounds great. If you will give us just a few minutes, we're going to meet and will be right with you. Would you mind waiting in the lobby?"

"Not at all." Cecelia gathered her things up into her portfolio and, with a smile, stepped out of the room. The moment she shut the door behind her she felt like a weight had been lifted from her shoulders. Somehow, having that wall between her and Deacon seemed to make a difference. Thankfully, his laser-like vision couldn't reach her through the drywall and the expensive wallpaper of Shane's offices.

No question, he had rattled her. He'd probably intended to. After everything she'd done to Deacon, she deserved it. For the first time, she started to doubt that she would land this job. Yes, Shane had personally approached her about it, but perhaps Deacon had agreed to it just so he could have the opportunity to reject her the way she'd rejected him all those years ago.

She poured herself a glass of water at the nearby beverage station and took a seat, waiting anxiously for their decision. She was surprised they were moving so quickly, but if they needed the hotel done by the end of the month, there really wasn't a choice. She was the last designer to present her ideas, so the time to decide was here.

About ten minutes later, the door opened and a flow of board members exited the room. Cecelia waited patiently until her name was called and then stepped back into the conference room. The only person left in there was Deacon. She struggled to maintain her professional composure as she waited for him to finally speak to her. Now that they were alone, she was expecting him to lay into her about why she didn't deserve the job.

Instead, he smiled politely and stuffed his hands into his pants pockets. "I won't prolong the torture, Ms. Morgan. The bottom line is that everyone is very pleased with your designs and the direction that you'd like to take for The Bellamy. Shane has gone upstairs to have our contracts department write up something, and we will have it couriered over to your offices as soon as it's ready. Presuming, of course, that you will accept the job."

She'd be crazy not to. The budget that Shane had discussed with her was more than enough to cover materials and labor expenses and provide a tidy profit for her to add to her company's bottom line. She and her team would be working hard to earn it, but the very future of Luna Fine Furnishings was riding on the success of this project. *No* simply wasn't an option. She didn't want to seem too eager, however, especially where Deacon was concerned. "I'm happy to hear that you're pleased. I look forward to reviewing the contracts and touching base with you and Shane."

He nodded. "I understand the schedule is a bit hectic. The ground floor of the hotel has a business suite with several offices available for future hotel management. We're happy to offer you an on-site office location to help you better manage your team and their progress."

That would help. Especially if there was a cot in it where she could sleep. Perhaps she could finish a room so she could stay in it. "That would be lovely, thank you." She hesitated a moment before she spoke again. "May I ask you something?"

Deacon raised his brow in curiosity. "Of course."

She knew she should take the offer and run, but she wanted to know why they'd chosen her. Why *he'd* chosen her. "I am very grateful for this opportunity, but I'm curious as to why you chose to go with me instead of an established design firm. I'm sure you're aware that I've specialized in nursery and children's furnishings for the last few years. This is my first foray in adult luxury design."

Deacon nodded and thought over his response.

"Shane and I requested your proposal because we knew the quality would be high. To the Moon is known for producing the best you can buy for a child's room. There's no reason for us to believe it would be any different with your adult designs. You're the best at whatever you choose to do, Cecelia. You always were."

There was a flicker of pain in his eyes as he spoke, but it was quickly masked by the return of his cold indifference to her. "If you'll excuse me," he said, before turning and marching quickly from the conference room.

Cecelia was left standing there, a little shell-shocked from their encounter. He said she was the best at what she did, but she could read between the lines—*except when it came to us*. She excelled in business but was a miserable failure when it came to love.

Deacon might be willing to hire her to do a job she was well capable of, but it was clear that he wasn't about to forgive her for what she'd done to him.

Deacon had made a mistake.

The minute Cecelia had strolled into that conference room, it had felt as though someone had punched him in the stomach. He'd tried to maintain the appearance of the confident, arrogant businessman, but on the inside he felt anything but. His chest was constricted, and he couldn't breathe. His heart was racing like he was in the middle of a marathon. He had thought he would be immune to her after all this time, but he was wrong.

Cecelia had been wearing a smart, tailored ivory-and-gold suit that accented every curve of her womanly figure. That certainly wasn't the body he remembered. She was still petite, but she had grown up quite a bit since he saw her last. He was still attempting to recover from the tantalizing glimpse of her cleavage at the V of her blouse when she smiled at him and flipped her long blond curls casually over her shoulder.

Instantly, he knew he was lost.

What the hell was he thinking coming back here? And an even better question, why had he insisted that Shane give Cecelia the opportunity to compete for the design job? He had all but guaranteed that he would come face-to-face with her like this. It was a terrible idea.

Cecelia had begun her presentation talking about fabrics and furniture details he really didn't give a damn about. He'd hardly heard a word she said. His mind was clouded with the scent of her perfume, reminding him of hot nights in the back of his pickup truck. It was the same scent she'd worn in high school. He'd had to save up for two months to be able to afford a bottle of it for her birthday.

Now all he could think about was her naked, willing body sprawled out beneath his own, his nose buried in her throat, drawing her scent deep into his lungs. They had dated for only six months during their senior year, but they had been some of the best months of his life. Deacon hadn't been sure what he was going to do with his life or if he was ever going to make something of himself, but he instantly knew that he wanted Cecelia to be a part of his future. He couldn't remember how many times they'd made love, but he knew it hadn't been enough.

Looking at her during the presentation, as she'd gestured toward a watercolor rendering of a guest suite, all he could see was the younger Cecelia sitting on his tailgate smiling at him.

Suddenly, every muscle in his body had tensed, every nerve firing sparks of need through him. Occasionally, Cecelia's gaze would flick over him and his throat threatened to close. He'd gripped the arm of his executive chair, trying to ground himself and calm down. It had been no way to act during a professional board meeting. If she had finished her briefing early, he wouldn't have been able to stand up to thank her without embarrassing himself.

Deacon thought that returning to Royal as a successful real estate developer would change things. But every ounce of cockiness and confidence seemed to fly out the window the moment he'd laid eyes on Cecelia. Suddenly, he was an awkward teenager again. His old insecurities washed over him. He hadn't been good enough for her then, and for some reason he didn't feel good enough for her even now.

Of course, it hadn't helped that their last conversation on graduation night had been her breaking up with him. He didn't know exactly what had made her change her mind. Up until that point, she'd been very enthusiastic about their plans and their future together. Then, suddenly, she'd turned a one-eighty on him and walked away.

Deacon had always known he wasn't the kind of boy the Morgans wanted for their daughter. He didn't come from a good family, he was poor and he worked with his hands. He was certain that Brent and Tilly were thrilled that Cecelia had chosen someone like Chip Ashford, former captain of the football team, Texas senator, son of one of the most respected and wealthy families in Houston. He had a bright future ahead of him, no doubt.

Damn him for putting himself in this position, knowing he would be drawn to Cecelia as he always had been, but once again unable to have what he wanted.

He had to remind himself that he hadn't returned

to Royal to seduce Cecelia. That wasn't why he'd asked her to do this presentation, either. He had come back to prove to her, and everyone else in the small-minded little town, that he was better than them. To show them that he could take his humble beginnings and still manage to create an empire faster than any of them could manage to inherit. He'd come back to make Cecelia regret her decision. To make the Morgans regret their decision. Nothing more.

When he completed his mission and opened his new hotel, Deacon would return to Europe, indulge his vices and forget all about the cliquish and unimportant people of Royal, Texas.

Well, he doubted he'd forget about Cecelia.

He'd only *thought* it was hard being around Cecelia while she did her presentation. Being alone with her had been agonizing. What was he going to do now that she would be working at his hotel nonstop until it opened? He wouldn't be able to get away from her even if he wanted to. And he didn't.

He felt like an idiot as he strolled down the hallway to the office Shane had provided for him while he was in town. He felt like he'd run away from Cecelia. He should've been more confident, indifferent, as though she'd had no impact on him at all.

Just as he sat down at his desk, Shane appeared in his doorway. "A successful day, I'd say! We not only have a hotel, but the guests won't be sleeping on the floor. What do you say we go down to the Texas Cattleman's Club and celebrate with a drink?"

Deacon arched a brow at his friend. He'd never set foot in that building before. He hadn't even been good enough to clean their pool back in high school. "I'm not a member," he pointed out. "And I'm sure there are plenty of people in the club who would see to it that I never get to be one of them."

Shane dismissed him. "You are certainly welcome as my guest. And if you really wanted to be in the club I could sponsor you. I'm sure few people would have the nerve to speak up against me. Lately, the uproar has been more about the Maverick scandals, and I'm pretty sure that doesn't involve you. Aside from that, there are still a few folks sore that women can become members of the club. You should've heard some of the bitching when the billiards room was converted to a day care. I'm sure they'd be happy to admit you and counteract the appearance that it's turning into a henhouse instead of a clubhouse."

Deacon had never entertained the idea of joining the club. And all things considered, he really didn't want anything to do with an organization that had just decided in the past few years that women were worthy of participating. But he wouldn't be rude about it because he knew Shane was a member and enjoyed it. "No thanks. I think I'm going to finish up a few things here and call it a night. There is a T-bone steak in the fridge that's begging to be grilled tonight, and I can't disappoint it."

Shane smiled. "Okay, if you insist. But I'm going to drag you down there one day, though."

"Why? What's so great about a bunch of people sitting around in cowboy hats—which I don't own—talking about cattle and horses—which I'm not interested in?"

"Well, for one thing, the restaurant makes the finest steaks you'll ever eat. The bartenders pour a perfectly balanced dry martini. It's a nice place to hang out, have a drink and chat with friends."

Deacon supposed that to anyone else, it would sound very inviting. "Well, you're my only friend in town, so again, I'll pass. You go on and eat a finely prepared steak on my behalf."

Shane finally gave up, nodding and throwing up a hand in goodbye.

Deacon watched him go, relieved that he managed to get out of dinner. He had many reasons for avoiding the clubhouse, but the biggest one was Cecelia and Chip. He knew that both of them were members, and he had no interest in running into either of them tonight. Not after she'd spent the afternoon twisting his insides into knots.

No, he needed a little time before he saw Cecelia again. He needed to remind himself how badly she'd hurt him and how much he wanted her to regret what she'd done. To keep his head on straight, he had to stay away from her.

A steak, a stiff drink and a Netflix binge would do it.

He hoped.

Three

When Cecelia got back to her office later that afternoon, she found a giddy Simone waiting for her in the lobby. Cecelia loved Simone, she was one of her best friends in the whole world, but after the day she'd had—hell, after the week she'd had—she wasn't really in the mood. She had to jump on this Bellamy job right away if they were going to make the grand opening deadline.

Simone obviously didn't care, ignoring the stressed-out vibes Cecelia knew she was sending out. She followed Cecelia down the halls of To the Moon to her private office. "Have you heard the latest news?" Simone asked after she slipped into the room behind her.

Cecelia dropped her things down on her desk and plopped, exhausted, into her chair. "Nope. There's news?"

Simone rubbed her hands together in excitement and rushed over to sit on the edge of her desk. "So," she began, "word is that Maverick is at it again. A message went out on social media to everybody in the Texas Cattleman's Club today."

Cecelia held her breath as she waited to hear the latest news. She'd been too busy with The Bellamy project to check her phone. Had Maverick taken her money and spread her secret anyway? "So, what did the message say?"

Simone pulled her cell out of her purse and flipped through it to find the message. Locating it, she handed the phone over to Cecelia. The message was short and blessedly vague. It read: Someone in the Texas Cattleman's Club is not who they say they are.

Cecelia shrugged it off and handed the mobile back to Simone, feigning disinterest. "That's hardly big news. I'd say half the people there aren't who they pretend to be."

Simone returned her phone to her bag. "And to think that folks still believe we're the ones behind the attacks!"

"I have to say I'm thankful this last message went out when I couldn't possibly have sent it. I've got a room full of witnesses."

Simone just shrugged. "That doesn't mean they don't still think Naomi and I are the culprits, that we're all in on it together. If I had the time, I just might be the kind to do it. You've got to give the guy credit. Royal has been pretty dull lately. Maverick has brought more excitement to town in the last few months than we've had since the tornados hit."

Excitement? Cecelia certainly wouldn't consider extortion or extreme weather exciting. They were both terrifying in their own right. "You know, you might not want to act so excited when that stuff comes out. It makes us look guilty."

"Hey, I thought you would enjoy this more. What's wrong with you today? You don't seem like your usual self."

Cecelia wanted to shout, *"Because the real Maverick is blackmailing me! That message was about me!"* But she wouldn't. Instead she said, "I'm just stressed out and tired. I had that big presentation today at The Bellamy."

Simone perked up again. "So, how did it go? Did you dazzle Shane with your designs? Is he going to dump Brandee and run away with you? Please tell me that at the very least he wasn't rude."

"He was fine. And Brandee didn't even come

up. You could say that I dazzled him, since they offered me the contract. It seems I also dazzled his silent partner, Deacon Chase."

Simone's nose wrinkled in thought as she tried to place the name. "Deacon Chase. Why do I know that name?"

"Because," Cecelia explained, "that was my first boyfriend in high school."

Simone's eyes grew as wide as saucers. "Are you kidding me? Is *that* Deacon Chase Shane's silent partner? Didn't you lose your virginity to him?"

Cecelia looked around nervously to make sure that none of her employees overheard their discussion. Getting up from her chair, she ran to her office door and shut it. "Say it a little louder, Simone. Yes, Deacon was my first." Those weren't exactly helpful memories considering he was in town at the moment, but they were true. Deacon had been the first boy she ever loved. The last boy she'd ever loved.

"Does Chip know he's in town?"

"Does that matter?" Cecelia asked. "Chip and I didn't date in high school. We didn't even date in college. He's got no reason to worry about Deacon."

Simone wasn't convinced. "Yeah, but he knows you two dated and were pretty serious. You don't think it's going to bother him that Deacon is back in Royal?"

If there was only one thing that Cecelia knew

about Chip, it was that his ego was bigger than the state of Texas. In his opinion, Deacon was from a lower class of people. He wasn't competition in Chip's eyes, and never would be. "I don't think it would bother Chip. I mean, I agreed to marry Chip. I broke it off with Deacon after graduation, so I don't know why he would feel threatened by him."

Simone shook her head. "Chip may not have been threatened by the Deacon we knew back in high school, but if he is Shane's partner in the hotel, he's done well for himself. That may change things."

Cecelia wasn't sure about that, but she didn't really have time to worry. "Well, I'm sure that Deacon won't stay. He will be long gone once the hotel is finished. Speaking of Chip, I've got to get out of here. He and I are meeting for dinner tonight at the club. We're celebrating my new contract with the hotel."

"Excellent. I've really got to get out of here, too. I just stopped by on my way out of town to share the latest gossip. I'm meeting Naomi at the airport. We're flying out tonight to that fashion show in LA. We'll be there for a couple of days. You be sure to keep us posted if anything new happens with Maverick."

"I will, although I'm not sure you'd be so excited about his next attack if he were blackmailing *you*."

Cecelia certainly didn't feel that way now that she was his latest victim.

"Oh, I'm sure he'll get to me eventually. He'll get to all of us eventually."

Simone practically skipped out of Cecelia's office as if Maverick's threats didn't bother her. Cecelia hadn't been bothered, either, until a few days ago. Now the worry was front and center.

He had to be alluding to her in his latest message. She had wired the money the way her dad had instructed her to, and yet he hadn't backed off. It was exactly what she was afraid of. Once you stepped into the cycle of blackmail, there was no good way to get out of it. She wouldn't be surprised to see another message tonight asking for more money. Despite what her father had told her, Cecelia knew she had to use a different tact with Maverick.

Her parents didn't want her to tell Chip the truth, but that might be her only option if Maverick didn't back down. Chip's family was not only wealthy, but they had connections. If she confided her secret in him perhaps he could help to protect her. The Ashfords could crush Maverick like a bug...*if* they wanted to. She hoped they would, because she didn't know who else to turn to. She would have to tell him tonight at dinner before things got worse.

She was counting on him to be her savior.

* * *

Cecelia was a ball of nerves as she pulled her BMW into the parking lot of the Texas Cattleman's Club.

The club wasn't where she would've chosen to have this important discussion with Chip, but he had made the arrangements without asking her. Inside, she found Chip seated in the far corner booth of the dining room. She let the host escort her back to the table. Chip got up as she approached and gave her a short embrace and a chaste kiss on the cheek. "There you are, kitten. You're late. I was starting to worry."

Cecelia looked at her watch as she sat down and it was exactly five thirty. She wasn't about to argue with him, though. To Chip, if you didn't arrive five minutes early, you were late. "I'm sorry. I got hung up with Simone. She wanted to talk to me before she left for California with Naomi."

Chip settled into the booth across from her and smiled. "And what did the lovely Simone have to tell you today?"

Cecelia considered her words. "Well, I wanted to wait to talk to you about this until after we ordered."

"I already ordered for us both," Chip interjected. "I got you the grilled mahimahi since you're watching your weight for the wedding."

Cecelia tried to swallow her irritation. She hated when Chip made decisions for her. Especially when those decisions were based on imaginary weight she had no intention of losing, *thankyouverymuch*. It was a portent of her future with him that she tried hard to ignore. She feared she would be going from spending all her time trying to please her parents, to trying to please her husband.

"Then I suppose I don't have to wait," she said, ignoring his comments. "Simone told me that Maverick is blackmailing somebody new."

Chip nodded thoughtfully and accepted the gin and tonic the waiter brought him before placing a glass of white wine in front of Cecelia. "I saw something come up this afternoon, but I was too busy to pay much attention to it. What does that have to do with Simone? Is she his latest victim? I wouldn't be surprised if she got into some trouble."

Cecelia steeled her nerves, thankful for the glass of wine even though she would've preferred a red. She took a healthy sip before she started the discussion. "No, he's actually blackmailing me."

"What?" Chip shushed her, leaning into her across the table. "Not so loud, people will hear you." He scanned the dining area for anyone who might hear. Fortunately, it was still early for the dinner crowd at the club. The closest table was involved in a lively discussion about steer and not paying any attention to them. "What is going on?" he asked when he seemed certain it was safe to continue their discussion.

Cecelia followed suit, leaning in and speaking in low, hushed tones. "I got a message from him. It seems he found something out about me from a long time ago, and he's trying to blackmail me with it. Well, I supposed he's been successful since I've already made one payment to him, but it doesn't seem like it was enough, given the post this afternoon."

Chip's expression was stiff and stoic, without any of the sympathy or concern for her that she was hoping for. "What is he blackmailing you about? You told me you had a squeaky-clean past. It's absolutely critical, if you're going to be the wife of a senator, that you don't have anything in your life that can be detrimental to my career."

Cecelia sighed. How did this become about him and his career? "I know. It's not really something I think about very often. It was completely out of my control. My parents chose to keep it secret to protect me, but in the end, I don't think it's that bad. It's hardly a skeleton in my closet, Chip."

Chip eyed her expectantly, but she hesitated. She hadn't said the words out loud in thirteen years. Only ever said them once, the night she confided in Deacon. Somehow she wasn't sure this would go as well. "I'm adopted," she whispered.

Chip flinched as though she had slapped him across the face. "Adopted? Why didn't you tell me?"

Cecelia gritted her teeth at his reaction. She could already tell this was a mistake. "No one was ever to find out. I was adopted by the Morgans when I was only a few weeks old. They decided to raise me as their own child and have never told anybody about my history…because of who my mother was."

"What's wrong with your mother?"

"She had a drug problem. I was taken away from her when I was only two weeks old. My parents told me that she was so distraught, she overdosed not long after that."

A furious expression came over Chip's face. "Are you telling me that your mother was a junkie?"

There was no way to make that part go down easier. "I guess so. She was never a part of my life, but yes, my mother had a serious and deadly drug problem."

Chip didn't appear to even hear her words. "I cannot believe you would lie to me about something like this." He flushed an ugly red with anger. She'd never seen her polished and professional fiancé like this. "I thought you were like me. I thought you were from a good family and would make a perfect wife. But you're nothing but an impostor playing a role. How could you agree to marry me when you were keeping something like that a secret?"

Cecelia's jaw dropped open in shock. She thought he might be surprised by the news, maybe even concerned about the potential backlash, but she certainly didn't think that he would accuse her of deceiving him. "I am not an impostor, Chip Ashford. You have known me my whole life. I was raised by the Morgans in the same Houston suburb you were. I went to all the best schools like you did. I am nothing like my birth mother, and I never will be. I couldn't control who my mother was any more than you could."

Chip just shook his head. "You can dress it up, but a liar is always a liar."

Cecelia's blood ran cold in her veins. "Chip, please, don't be like this. I didn't intentionally deceive you. My parents just thought it was best that no one know."

"Thank goodness for Maverick," Chip said. "Without him I never would've found out the truth about you. You and your parents would've let me marry you knowing that everything I believed about you was a lie."

Her eyes welled up with tears she couldn't fight. Was Chip about to break up with her over this? She couldn't believe it, but that's what it sounded like. "Chip…"

"Don't," he snapped. "Don't look at me like that with tears in your eyes and try to convince me that you are a victim in this. I'm sorry, Cecelia, but the engagement is off. I can't marry somebody I can't trust. You're a liability to every future campaign I run, and I'm not about to destroy my career for a woman who is living a lie."

Cecelia looked down at the gigantic diamond-and-platinum ring that she'd worn for the past six months of their engagement. She hadn't particularly liked the ring, but she couldn't say so. It was gaudy, but it was as expected for someone of his station. She didn't want to keep it, not when his words were like a knife to the heart. She grasped it between her fingers and tugged it off her hand, handing it across the table.

Chip took it and stuffed it into his pocket. "Thank you for being reasonable about that."

At least one of them could be reasonable, she thought as the pain of his rejection slowly morphed into anger. She never would've confided in Chip if she'd known he would react like this. Now, all she could hope for was damage control. "I hope that I can still count on you to keep this secret," Cecelia said. "Odds are it will get out eventually, but I would prefer it to be on my terms if you don't mind. For my parents' sake."

Chip got up from the table and shrugged it off.

"What good would it do me to tell anybody? I've wasted enough time here. Have the waiter put dinner on my tab." He turned on his heel and marched out of the restaurant, leaving Cecelia to sit alone with their cocktails, a basket of bread sticks and an order for food they wouldn't even eat.

A hollow feeling echoed through her as she looked at his empty seat. Cecelia thought she would be more upset about her broken engagement, but she was just numb. The truth was that she didn't love Chip. Their relationship was more about strategic family connections than romance, but it still smarted to have him dump her like this when she was at her lowest point. They had planned a future together. They discussed how after The Bellamy deal they were going to sit down and make some solid wedding plans. Instead of finally getting one step closer to the family that she longed for, she was starting over.

Even if Chip kept his word and didn't spread her secret all over town, it would be embarrassing enough for everyone to find out about her broken engagement. Everyone would speculate about why they broke up if neither of them was talking. She wondered what Chip would tell them.

In the end, she was certain that her secret would come out anyway. One way or another everyone was going to find out that Cecelia was the adopted daughter of a junkie. Royal was a place where everybody was always in everyone else's business. They had all the drama and glamour that the Houston society provided, with all of the small-town nosiness that Cecelia could do without.

When the truth came to light, she wondered who would still be standing beside her. The members of the Texas Cattleman's Club were supposed to be like a family, but they were a fickle one.

Then there was the matter of her real family. How would her parents ever recover from the fallout? They'd built their lives on maintaining a perfect facade. Would their family, circle of friends and business contacts ever forgive the decades-long deception?

Reeling from the events of the evening, Cecelia picked up her purse and got up from the table, leaving a stack of bills to cover the tab. She could've let Chip pay for it all, but she didn't want to face the waiter and explain why she was suddenly alone with a tableful of food coming out of the kitchen.

As she got into her car, she leaned back against the soft leather seat and took a deep breath. At this moment, she needed her friends more than ever. But as Simone had said earlier, she and Naomi were already on a plane to California. They wouldn't be back for several days.

She couldn't talk to her parents about this. They

would be more distraught about her breakup with Chip than how painful this was for her. She loved her parents, but they were far more concerned with appearances than anything else. She was certain that when word of her broken engagement got around to them, she would get an earful. She could just imagine her mother scrambling to get back in the Ashfords' good graces.

At the moment, Cecelia didn't really give a damn about the Ashfords. If they couldn't accept her the way she was, she didn't want to marry into their family anyway. So what if she wasn't of the good breeding that Chip thought she was? She was still the same person he had always known. The woman he had proposed to.

As she pulled her car out of the parking lot of the club, she found herself turning left instead of right toward the Pine Valley subdivision where she lived in a French château-inspired home. There wasn't much to the left, but Cecelia was in desperate need of a stretch of road to drive and clear her mind.

After a few miles, she realized that maybe all this was for the best. Perhaps Maverick was doing her a favor in the end. It was better that she and Chip break up now, while they were still engaged, than to have a messy divorce on her hands. And God forbid they'd started a family. Would Chip reject his own children if he found out that they were tainted by their mother's inferior bloodline?

Cecelia shuddered at the thought. The one thing she wanted, the one thing she'd always wanted, was a family of her own. She longed for blood relatives whom she was bound to by more than just a slip of paper. People who would love her without stipulations and requirements. Her parents did love her, of that she had no doubt. But the Morgans' high standards were hard to live up to. She had always strived to meet them, but lately she wondered how they would feel about her if she fell short. Would they still love and protect their perfect Cecelia if she wasn't so perfect?

As she made her way to the edge of town, she noticed lights on in the distance at the old Wilson House and slowed her car to investigate. She didn't realize anybody had bought that property. No one had lived in the large, luxurious cabin for several years, but someone was definitely there now.

She wasn't sure why she did it, but she turned her car down the winding gravel road that led to the old house. Maybe it was Maverick's secret hideout. There, out front, she spied a fully restored 1965 Corvette Stingray convertible roadster. She knew nothing of cars, but she remembered a poster of one almost exactly like this on Deacon's bedroom wall in high school. That one had been cherry red—his dream car.

This one was a dark burgundy, but she knew the moment she saw it that the car belonged to Deacon. Instantly, she realized there was no place else she wanted to be in the whole world.

Deacon had known the truth about her. Years ago when they were in high school and completely infatuated with one another, they had confessed all their secrets. Cecelia had told him about her adoption and about her mother. She had even shown him the only picture she had of her mother. The old, worn photograph, given to her by her parents on her thirteenth birthday, had been found in her mother's hand when she died. It was a picture of her holding her brand-new baby girl, just a week before she was taken away.

Cecelia had spent a lot of time staring at that photo, looking for the similarities between her and her mother. Looking for the differences that made her better. She'd always been mystified by her mother's happy smile as she held her baby. How could she throw that all away? Every now and then she pulled the photo out to look at it when she was alone. Deacon hadn't judged her. Deacon had accepted her for who she was—the rich, spoiled daughter of the Morgan family and the poor, adopted daughter taken away from her drug-addled mother. Deacon had loved her just the same.

In this moment, she wanted nothing more than to feel that acceptance again. Without thinking, she drove up to the front of the house and got out of her car. She flew up the steps and knocked on the front door, not knowing what his reaction would be when he saw her. Judging by their interaction earlier that day, she didn't expect a warm welcome.

But she didn't care.

A moment later, the large door opened wide, revealing Deacon standing there in nothing but a pair of worn blue jeans. She had admired his new build during her briefing that day, but she could only guess what he was hiding beneath his designer suit. Now his hard, chiseled physique was on display, from his firm pecs to his defined six-pack. His chest and stomach were sprinkled with golden-brown chest hair she didn't remember from their times together in the past. Her palms itched to run her hands across him and see how different he felt.

Then her eyes met his, and the light of attraction and appreciation flickered there. Cecelia felt a surge of desire and bravery run through her, urging her on, so she didn't hesitate.

Before Deacon could even say hello, Cecelia launched herself into his arms.

Four

The last thing Deacon expected when he opened his front door was to find Cecelia standing there. If he had suspected that, perhaps he would've put a shirt on. Or perhaps not.

Instead, he'd been standing there half-naked when he opened the door and looked into the seductive gray eyes of his past. She'd seemed broken somehow, not as confident as she'd been during her earlier presentation. She'd appeared to almost tremble as her eyes glistened with unshed tears. Before he could ask what was wrong, or why she was here, she'd launched herself at him, and was kissing him.

At that point all Deacon could do was react. And in that moment, with the woman he had once loved in his arms again after all this time, he couldn't push her away. Their encounter that afternoon had only lit the fires of his need for her once again. The years of anger and resentment took a back seat to desire, at least for the moment. He had no idea what had brought her to his doorstep tonight, but he was thankful for it.

Now her mouth was hot and demanding as she continued to kiss him. These were nothing like the sweet, hesitant kisses of their teenage years. Cecelia was a grown woman who knew exactly what she wanted and how to get it. And from the looks of it, she wanted Deacon.

She buried her fingers in the hair at the nape of his neck, pulling him closer as she pressed her body against his bare chest. He could feel the globes of her full breasts molding against the hard wall of his chest through the thin silk of the blouse he had admired earlier that day. As her tongue slipped into his mouth, he felt a growl form in the back of his throat. She certainly knew how to coax the beast out of him. He tried not to think about how Chip Ashford could've been the one to teach her these new tricks.

That was the thought that yanked Deacon away from Cecelia's kiss. He took a step back, bracing her shoulders and holding her away from him. "What are you doing here, Cecelia?" he asked. "Shouldn't you be making out with your rich fiancé right now, instead of me?"

Cecelia silently held up her hand, wiggling the bare finger that had previously held the gigantic diamond he'd noticed that afternoon at the presentation. So, that meant the engagement was off, and just since he'd seen her last. That was an interesting development, although one he was certain had little to do with his arrival in town. Only in his fantasies would Cecelia cast aside Chip for him.

"May I come in?" she asked, looking up at him through thick, golden lashes.

His tongue snaked out over his lips as he nodded. "Sure." He took a step back, wondering what could've broken the engagement and driven Cecelia back into his arms, but before he could ask, she was on him again.

This time he had no reason to stop her. They stumbled back through the doorway, and he kicked it shut behind them. Without hesitation, he lifted Cecelia and started carrying her toward the bedroom. She clung to him, unwilling to separate her lips from his as he navigated through the house.

When they reached his bedroom, he sat her gently down at the edge of his king-size bed. Cecelia immediately started undoing his belt, sliding it from his jeans and tossing it to the floor. There was no question that this was what she wanted. And frankly, if he were being honest with himself, it was what he wanted, too.

He certainly didn't expect it to be dropped into his lap like this, but only a fool would ask questions instead of accepting the gift he'd been given. As she started to unbutton his pants, he reached for her hand and pulled it away.

"I've got this," he said.

Cecelia just smiled and began to undo her own blouse, button by button, exposing more of the creamy, porcelain skin he'd always admired. She was one of the few women he'd ever met who truly had a flawless complexion. There were no freckles, no moles—not even a scar. The Morgans would never allow their precious daughter to be injured. Her skin was like that of a china doll—smooth… even…perfect.

He remembered running his hands over it years ago and it feeling like silk against the rough, calloused palms he'd earned from working on cars. As she slipped her blouse off her shoulders and exposed the ivory satin of her bra, he ached to touch it and the flesh beneath it.

Her breasts nearly overflowed the cups as she breathed hard with wanting him. He took a step back as she stood to unzip her pencil skirt. The fabric slid over her ample hips and pooled at her feet. The sight of her nearly nude stole his breath away. She was just as beautiful and perfect as he remembered. Only now, she was a fully grown woman with all the curves that a man at his age could finally appreciate. As a teenager, Cecelia had been his first, and he'd hardly known what he was doing. He wouldn't have been able to handle a woman like Cecelia back then.

Cecelia's steely-gray eyes were fixed on him as she reached behind herself and unlatched her bra. Her breasts spilled free, revealing tight, strawberry-pink tips that were just as he remembered them. Thirteen years was too long to wait, and he couldn't resist reaching out to cup them in his hands. The hard peaks of her nipples pressed into his palms as he squeezed and massaged her sensitive flesh.

Cecelia sighed with contentment, leaned into his touch, tipped her head back and shook her blond waves over her shoulders. "Yes," she whispered. "I need your touch, Deacon. I need it now more than ever."

Deacon didn't respond. Instead, he dipped his head and took one of her tight buds into his mouth. He teased at it with his tongue until Cecelia was gasping and writhing against him. He wrapped his arm around her waist, holding her body tight against his, and then slipped one hand beneath her silky ivory panties.

He was surprised to find her skin completely bare and smooth there, providing no barrier for his fingers to slip between her sensitive folds and stroke her center. Cecelia gasped and her hips bucked against his hand, but he didn't stop. Instead he drew harder on her nipple, stroking her again and again until she came apart in his arms.

Cecelia cried out and clawed at his shoulders, more wild and passionate beneath him than she'd ever let herself be. She had gotten in touch with her sexuality, and he was pleased to be benefiting from it.

When her body stilled and her cries subsided, he lowered her gently onto the bed, laying her back against the brocade comforter. She watched beneath hooded eyes as he unbuttoned his jeans and slipped them off, along with the rest of his clothing. She watched him with appreciation as he sought out a condom from the nightstand and returned to where her body was sprawled across his mattress. He set the condom beside her on the bed, using both hands to grasp her panties and slide the fabric over her hips and down her legs.

With her completely exposed in front of him, Deacon could only shake his head in wonder. How had he gotten to this place tonight? He had anticipated grilling a steak on the back porch, drinking a few beers and watching the news. Instead, he would gladly go without his dinner and feast on Cecelia instead.

He opened the condom and rolled it down his length and then crawled onto the bed, positioning himself between her still-quivering thighs.

This was the moment he'd waited for, fantasized about, since the day he and Cecelia had parted ways. The last time they'd made love had been the night before their high school graduation. He'd had no idea that the next day Cecelia would be breaking up with him. He'd had no idea that he was holding her for the last time, kissing her for the last time, until it was too late. Then, all he could do was long for what he lost and search for it in the arms of other women.

"Please," Cecelia begged. "Don't make me wait any longer."

Deacon was more than happy to fulfill her wish. He slowly surged forward, pressing into her warmth until he was fully buried inside her. He gritted his teeth, fighting to keep control, as her tight muscles wrapped around him. She felt as good as he remembered. Maybe better.

Cecelia drew her knees up, wrapping her legs around his hips and holding him close. She reached up for him, cupping his face in her hands and drawing his mouth down to her own. He began to move, slowly at first, and then picking up speed. Her soft cries and groans of pleasure were muffled by his mouth against hers.

It didn't take long for the tension to build up inside him. Cecelia was eager and hungry for him, and he was near his breaking point. He moved harder and faster as she clawed at his back. The sharp sting was a painful reminder that although he was enjoying this, he needed to remember who he was with. The Cecelia of his past, of his fantasies, was long gone. The woman beneath him was harder, shrewder and lacking the sweet innocence he'd always associated with her.

No matter what he tried to tell himself, Deacon knew that she was just using him. Whatever had happened between her and Chip tonight had driven her into his arms. She probably wanted to forget about everything that was going wrong in her life and was using Deacon as a reminder of when things were better. It had worked. Whatever tensions and worries she'd arrived with on his doorstep were gone.

Admittedly, his mood had improved, too. As Deacon focused on the soft warmth of her body, the stress of the day melted away and a new kind of tension took its place. Cecelia's cries grew louder beneath him, signaling that she was close to another release. He wasn't far behind her. Reaching between them, he stroked her center, pushing her over the edge once again.

"Deacon!" she cried out, writhing under him.

The tightening of her muscles around him drew him closer to his release. He thrust into her three more times, hard and fast, and it was done. His jaw dropped open with a silent scream as he poured himself into her willing body.

When it was over, Deacon pulled away from her and flopped back onto the bed. Staring up at his ceiling, he had a hard time believing everything that had just happened. He'd come back to Royal in the hopes that Cecelia might regret dumping him all those years ago.

This was way better.

Cecelia awoke with a start. She sat up in bed, her heart racing in her chest, as she looked around the unfamiliar room. For a moment, she couldn't figure out where she was, but the morning light streaming across the furniture and the shape of the man in bed beside her pieced it together.

Suddenly everything came back to her at once. She'd slept with Deacon. No, she'd thrown herself at Deacon and he'd had the courtesy not to turn her down and make her look like a fool. What was she thinking, running to him like that? Of all the people in Royal?

Then again, who else did she have to turn to? She couldn't blame last night on alcohol, but apparently the emotional trauma of her breakup with Chip was enough to dull her inhibitions. With the arrival of dawn, her good sense returned to her, and she realized that last night, however amazing, had been a terrible mistake.

She pulled back the blankets and slipped silently from the bed. She crept through the room, collecting her clothing, and carried it with her to the hallway, where she pulled the bedroom door closed behind her and got dressed.

She looked back at the door and pictured the man asleep beyond it only once before she disappeared down the hallway and out the front door. She practically held her breath until she had started her car and made it down the driveway without Deacon showing up at his front door to see her leave. It was better this way. Neither of them had to face the reality of last night and what it meant, which was a big nothing.

They were both under stress, and the sex had done its job and gotten it out of their systems. Hopefully, she would be able to finish her work at The Bellamy without this becoming a problem for her. She had enough to deal with, with the fallout of her broken engagement and the threat of Maverick looming overhead. She didn't need any weird sexual tension buzzing between them while she was trying to pull off the design coup of the century.

Two hundred and fifty guest suites in less than a month was no laughing matter. It would take all of Cecelia's focus and drive to make it happen. She didn't have time for any distractions in her life, but she most certainly didn't need Deacon, who would be at the hotel every day, reminding her of what they'd just done while she tried to work.

And yet, by the time she reached Pine Valley Estates, she was feeling guilty about running out. That was no way to treat Deacon, especially after how welcoming he'd been last night. He'd had every right to slam the door in her face when she showed up at his doorstep without warning. She was the one who had broken up with him because he wasn't good enough for her. How dare she just show up and throw herself into his arms and expect him to welcome her? And yet he had.

Now she felt worse than ever.

She pulled her car into the garage at her château just around the time her alarm normally would wake her. There was no time for her to dwell on her mistakes. She needed to shower, change, grab a double-shot latte and get to work on her first day of The Bellamy project.

Cecelia made a stop at her office to collect the things she would need while she was working at the resort. With her laptop bag slung over her shoulder and a small file box of necessary paperwork and designs in hand, she headed back out to the receptionist's desk.

Her secretary, Nancy, was sitting there when she arrived. "Good morning, Miss Morgan," she said.

"Good morning, Nancy. Mr. Delgado and Mr. Chase graciously offered me an office at the hotel so I can oversee our work there over the next few weeks. Tell anyone who needs to get a hold of me that I have my cell phone and my computer."

Nancy jotted the note on the paper pad beside her. She waved as Cecelia turned and went out the front door with her things.

By the time Cecelia arrived at The Bellamy, work was in full swing for the day. She spied her painting team's truck, which meant that they were already laying a coat of steely-gray paint on the walls of every suite. By the time they were done, the wallpaper should have arrived and be ready to go on the accent walls and in the bathrooms.

She gathered up her things and started up the walkway into the back of the hotel, passing landscapers as they planted trees and bushes nearby. Inside she found an organized-looking woman in a headset and asked for directions. She pointed her down a hallway to the business suite of the hotel. There, she found one office designated for each of the owners, one for the hotel manager, one for the reservations manager, one for the catering manager and one empty office that had yet to be assigned. She assumed that would be hers for now.

She opened the door and turned on the light, finding a nicely appointed office space. She hadn't been contracted to decorate the interior management rooms, but it wouldn't be necessary. There was a desk, a rolling chair and a bookshelf. That was more than she would need while she was here. She busied herself unpacking her things and getting ready to dig into her work.

Once she was up and running, she started her day by making important calls. All of her suppliers needed to know that she had won the project bid and the pending orders needed to go forward as planned. Fabric, furniture and wallpaper were just the beginning. She had orders for paintings to go up in every single room, 250 matching small lamps to go on each nightstand, along with another 250 torch lamps for the corner behind the reading chair. Thousands of feet of carpeting needed to be ordered, in addition to ceramic tiles for the bathroom floors.

And all that needed to get here as soon as possible. As in yesterday.

Cecelia was lost in the minutiae of managing her inventory and orders when her cell phone rang. She looked down and noticed it was Naomi calling from California. She picked up the phone and answered it. "Hey, girl, how's California?"

"It's beautiful here," she said. "The weather is unreal. It makes me never want to come back to Texas, but of course I will, because you and Simone would kill me if I didn't."

"Is everything set up for the fashion show?"

Naomi just groaned. "I really don't want to talk about it. There's always last-minute chaos at these things. I didn't call to talk about all that anyway. I called because I got a text about you and Chip breaking up yesterday. Is that true?"

Cecelia had been hoping it would take longer for the news to get out, but apparently it was already making Royal's gossip rounds. "Yes, we've broken up, but really it's for the best. I think we just had different ideas of what our future was going to be."

"Hmm. So it didn't have anything to do with a *certain someone* coming back to town?"

Cecelia rolled her eyes. Simone must've told her about her run-in with Deacon. "No, it had nothing to do with him. I honestly doubt Chip even knows he's here yet. I didn't mention it."

"So what set all this off?"

She hesitated. She knew that she would eventually tell Naomi and Simone about her little black-mail problem, but now wasn't the time. "It was bound to happen eventually. Things just boiled over at dinner last night, so we called off the engagement. I'll tell you and Simone more about it when you get home. I wish you two were here."

"I'm so sorry that all this happened while we were gone, Cece. You've broken off your engagement and your two best friends aren't there to commiserate with you. That really sucks. I promise that when we get back, we will get together for some wine, a couple cartons of Ben & Jerry's and some good girl time. You'll put this whole thing behind you before you know it."

That sounded great. Cecelia really needed her friends to talk to. Had they been in town last night, perhaps she wouldn't have found herself in Deacon's bed.

"Good luck with the show," Cecelia said.

"Thank you. Hang in there. Oh, and don't forget that Wes and Isabelle's engagement party is coming up. You're not getting out of it, you know."

Oh, she knew. Cecelia said goodbye and got off the phone. She needed to remember to pick up a gift for that. Frankly, she had been surprised to receive the invitation, but Isabelle was the kind of woman who wanted to be friends with everybody, even the girl who had spilled the beans about her secret daughter and upended her whole life.

She had RSVP'd two weeks ago, but now she was regretting it. She didn't really want to stroll into the Texas Cattleman's Club and have to face everybody after the breakup. More than a few people there would get a sick amount of pleasure from her misfortune. But she said she would go, so she would go.

Cecelia had just turned back to her computer when she heard a tap at the door. She looked up and immediately felt a surge of panic run through her. Deacon was standing in her doorway, a look of expectation and irritation on his face. She'd been hoping, in vain, apparently, that he would be too busy to come looking for her this morning. "Good morning, Mr. Chase. What can I do for you?"

Deacon arched a curious brow at her and just shook his head. "So this is how it's going to be, huh? It never happened?"

Cecelia smiled, putting on her most business-like face as she tried to ignore the rough stubble on his jaw that she'd brushed her lips across only hours earlier. Her fingers tingled with the memory of running through his golden-blond hair and pulling him close to her. "I always like to keep things professional in the workplace."

"And later, when we're not in the workplace?" he asked.

"There's not much to say about last night, now or later, except that I apologize for the way I acted. It was inappropriate of me to burden you with my problems. After Chip broke off the engagement, I wasn't sure where to go or what to do. I made the wrong choice, and I'm sorry."

Deacon's green-gold gaze flickered over her face, studying her as though he could see the truth there. His jaw tightened, and finally he looked away. "The head of your painting crew is looking for you. He's waiting in the lobby."

Cecelia watched as Deacon turned and disappeared from her doorway without another word. The warm, attentive Deacon from last night was gone, leaving only the cold businessman behind. She hated that it had to be that way, and she wished he could understand. Now, more than ever, she needed his warmth and his compassion. All too soon, the rest of Royal would be turning their backs on her. But there was too much history between them, too many memories and emotions to cloud the present. She knew she had to put up a wall to protect her business and her reputation.

And her heart.

Five

He was a damn fool for thinking that their night together would go down any differently than it had.

Deacon knew better. He knew better than to just fall in the bed with Cecelia and think that things had changed. Just as before, he was good enough when they were alone, but not in public. He had thought that perhaps he had proved his worth, and that maybe things would go differently between them this time. Not so.

It had been a week since she'd shown up on his doorstep. They'd danced around each other at the hotel each day, both seemingly drawn to, and repelled by, each other. Cecelia avoided eye contact and stuck strictly to topics about work. But as hard as she tried to play it cool, it didn't change the underlying energy that ran through all of their interactions.

He wasn't about to give her the satisfaction of him chasing after her, however. The teenager whose heart she'd broken would've chased her anywhere if he thought he could have another chance. Real estate billionaire Deacon Chase didn't follow women around like a lost puppy dog.

But if there was one thing Deacon had learned in the past week, it was that she didn't regret that night. Not even one teensy, tiny, little bit. He'd seen the way her cheeks flushed when she'd looked up and seen him standing nearby. She had been hungry for the pleasure he happily gave her. That kind of hunger was nothing to be remorseful about. She'd come to him that night because she wanted to forget what a mess her life was for a little while, and he'd delivered in spades. More than likely, she regretted that she didn't regret their encounter.

Deacon hadn't lost too much sleep over it. They'd had sex. Amazing, mind-blowing sex, but just sex. It'd been thirteen years since they'd gotten together. They weren't in love with one another, and it was ridiculous to think that they ever would be. It would've been nice if she had said goodbye as she crept naked from his bedroom, but he supposed it had saved them from an awkward morning together.

No, what had bothered him the most during the past week was seeing who Cecelia had become over the years. Despite his feelings about her and their breakup, he had still loved the girl Cecelia had been. She'd been the sweetest, most caring person he had ever known outside of his own family. When the rest of the school, and the rest of the town, had turned their back on Deacon, Cecelia had been there.

The woman he watched stomping back and forth through the lobby of his hotel in high heels and a tight hair bun was not the Cecelia he remembered. She was driven, focused, almost to the point of being emotionless. What happened to her? When they had shared their dreams for the future as teenagers, being a hard-nosed CEO had not been on Cecelia's list of ambitions.

If he looked closely, every now and then Deacon could see a flicker of the girl he used to know. It was usually near the end of the day, when the stress and the worries started to wear her down. That was when her facade would start to crumble and he could see the real Cecelia underneath.

He was watching her like that when Shane approached him. "She's quite a piece of work, isn't she?"

Deacon turned to him, startled out of his thoughts. "What do you mean?"

"I've always thought that Cecelia was a victim of a contradictory modern society. If she were a man, everyone would applaud her for her success and uncompromising attitude in the boardroom. Since she's a woman, she's seen as cold and bitchy. Heck, I see her that way after the way she treated Brandee. But there's no way she could've gotten this far in business if she wasn't hard."

"You make it sound like nobody likes her." That surprised Deacon, since she'd been the most popular, outgoing person in high school. Everyone had loved her.

"Well, she has earned quite the reputation in Royal over the years. Aside from her few close friends, I'm not sure that anybody really likes her, especially inside the Texas Cattleman's Club. Tell you what, though, it's not for their lack of trying. She's just not interested in being friends with most people. She and the rest of the mean girl trio tried to sabotage my relationship with Brandee. They thought it was a big joke. I don't know if folks are just not good enough to be her friends or what."

Deacon flinched. "That doesn't sound like her at all. What the hell happened after I left town?"

"I don't know, man." Shane shrugged. "Maybe you broke her heart."

Deacon swallowed a bitter chuckle. "Don't you mean the other way around? She's the one who broke up with me."

"Yeah, well, maybe she regrets it. I certainly would rather date you over Chip Ashford any day."

"Aw, that's sweet of you, Shane."

"You know what I mean," Shane snapped. "I'd be a bitter, miserable woman if I were dating him, too. I'm curious as to what will happen to her socially, now that she's broken it off with Chip, though. A lot of people in town tolerated her and her attitude just because she was his fiancée."

The discussion of her broken engagement caught Deacon's attention. "So do you know exactly what happened between her and Chip?"

Shane just shook his head. "I haven't heard anything about it, aside from the fact that it's over. It seems both of them are keeping fairly tight-lipped about the whole thing, which is unusual. I have heard that her parents are beside themselves about the breakup. They've been kissing the Ashfords' asses for years to get in their good graces, and I'm sure they think Cecelia has ruined it for them."

It grated on Deacon's nerves that Cecelia's parents were always more worried about appearances than they were about their own daughter. Couldn't they see that she was miserable with Chip? Probably so. They just didn't care. Deacon had never thought much of their family. They acted like they were better than everyone else. "Who cares about the Ashfords?" he asked.

"Everybody," Shane said before turning and wandering off, disappearing as suddenly as he had arrived.

Deacon watched him go, and then he turned back to where Cecelia had been standing a moment before. She was barking orders at a crew of men hauling in rolls of carpeting. When she was finished, she turned and headed in his direction with her tablet clutched in her arms. He braced himself for a potentially tense conversation, but she didn't even make eye contact. She breezed past him as though he were invisible and disappeared down the hallway.

A cold and indifferent bitch, indeed.

Looking down at his watch, Deacon realized he couldn't spend all of his time staring at Cecelia. The hotel opening was in a little more than three weeks, and they had a ton of work ahead of them. That was why he had returned to Royal after all— well, the official reason anyway. He turned on his heel and headed back toward his office to get some work done before the end of the day arrived.

When he looked up from his computer next it

was after seven. It was amazing how time could get away from him while he was working. He couldn't imagine doing this job and having a family to go home to every night. He imagined he would have a very angry wife and very cold dinners. He stood up, stretched and reached over to turn off his laptop.

He switched off the light as he stepped out of his office, noticing the business suite was dark except for one other space. Cecelia's office. As quietly as he could, he crept down the hallway to peer in and see what she was doing here this late.

Cecelia was sitting in her chair with her back to him, but she wasn't working. She was looking at something in her hand. Deacon took a few steps closer so he could make out what it was. Finally, he could tell it was an old, worn photograph. One that he recognized.

She'd shown him the photo the night she confessed her biggest secret: that she was adopted. It was of a young woman, weary and worn but happy, holding a new baby. It was a picture of Cecelia's birth mother on the day she brought her daughter home from the hospital. Deacon hadn't given much thought to the photo back then. He had been more interested in Cecelia and the way she talked about it. She had always seemed conflicted about her birth mother. It was as though she wanted to know her, wanted to learn more about who she had been and why she had gotten so lost, and yet she was embarrassed by where she had come from. Deacon had no doubt that she had the Morgans to thank for that.

There was a lot going on with Cecelia. More than just regret over their one-night stand. More than just missing her mother. More than just being upset over her broken engagement. There was something else going on that she wasn't telling him. The whole town was convinced she was just a stuck-up mean girl, but he'd bet not one of them had looked hard enough to see that she was hurting. Of course, she had no reason to confide in him. While he'd proved himself trustworthy in the past, they weren't exactly close anymore. In that moment it bothered him more than in the thirteen years they'd been apart.

He wanted to go into her office and scoop her up into his arms. Not to kiss her. Not to carry her away and ravish her somewhere, but just to hold her. He got the feeling that it was a luxury Cecelia could barely afford. Chip didn't seem like a supportive, hold-his-woman kind of guy, and that was exactly what she needed right now.

But did he dare?

She had done nothing but avoid him since their night together. She'd made it crystal clear that she didn't want any sort of relationship with Deacon, sexual or otherwise. She just wanted to do her job, and so he would let her. The last thing he needed was to leave Royal for the second time with a broken heart and a bruised ego.

As quietly as he could, Deacon took a few steps back and disappeared down the hallway so he didn't disturb her. As he stepped out into the parking lot, there were only two cars remaining—his Corvette and her BMW. He stopped beside her car and stared down at it for a moment, thinking. Finally, he fished a blank piece of scrap paper out of his pocket and scribbled a note on it before placing it under her windshield wiper.

"I'm here if you need to talk—Deacon," it read.

Whether or not she would take him up on it, he had no idea. But he hoped so.

Things had been hard for Cecelia the past couple of weeks. She tried to lose herself in her work and forget about everything that was going wrong in her life, but in the evenings at the hotel, when it was calm and quiet, she had nothing to distract her from the mess of her own making.

Earlier that night, she'd gotten another message from Maverick. As she'd expected, the original payment was just that, and not nearly enough to keep him quiet. Another twenty-five thousand had to be wired by the end of the week, or her secret would be out and her family would be humiliated. Staring at the photo of her mother, she'd quietly decided that she wasn't giving him any more money. She felt a pang of guilt where her parents were concerned—surely they would face an uphill battle in restoring the trust of those they lied to—but it was time for her to take control of her life. Come what may.

Now, sitting in her car in the long-empty parking lot of the hotel, she clutched what might be her only lifeline. Finding the note on her windshield from Deacon had been a surprise. They hadn't really spoken since the morning she ran out on him, aside from the occasional discussion about the hotel. She thought she was doing a good job at keeping her worries inside, but Deacon had seen through it somehow. He'd always had that ability. In some ways, that made him someone she needed to avoid more than ever. In other ways, he was just the person she needed to talk to. The only person she could talk to.

But could she take him up on his offer?

At this point, she didn't have much to lose. Before she could second-guess herself, she put her car in Drive and found herself back on the highway that led to Deacon's place. Her heart was pounding in her chest with anxiety as she drove up the gravel path through the trees. His car was there, and the lights were on inside. Hopefully he was there alone.

She bit anxiously at her lip as she rang the doorbell and waited. This time, when Deacon answered the door, he was fully dressed in the suit he'd worn to the hotel that day, and she was able to control herself. Barely. "Hi," she said. It seemed a simple, silly way to start such a heavy conversation, but she didn't know what else to say.

Deacon seemed to sense how hard it was for her to accept his olive branch. Instead of gloating, he just took a step back and opened the door wider to let her inside.

"You said you were here if I needed to talk. Is this a good time?"

Deacon shut the door and turned to her with a serious expression lining his face. His green-gold eyes reflected nothing but sincerity as he looked at her and said, "Whenever you need to talk to me, I will make the time."

Cecelia was taken aback by the intensity of his words and their impact on her. She never felt like she was anybody's priority, especially Chip's. He always had an important meeting, a campaign to run, a fund-raiser to plan, hands to shake and babies to kiss. Cecelia had been an accessory to him, like a nice suit or pair of cuff links. "Thank you," was all she could say.

Deacon led her through the foyer and into his sunken great room. The space was two stories high with a fireplace on the far end that went all the way to the ceiling with stacked gray-and-brown flag-stone. He gestured for her to sit in the comfortable-looking brown leather sectional that was arranged around a coffee table made of reclaimed wood and glass. It was very much a cowboy's living room, reminding her of the clubhouse.

"Are you renting this place?" she asked.

"No, I actually went ahead and bought it. It was a good deal, and it came furnished. That made it easier for me to settle in and gave me a real home to come to each night. Despite the fact that I build hotels for a living, I don't exactly relish living in one. When the hotel is finished, I'll return to France, but I'll probably keep this place. Shane will be over-seeing the business operations, but I'll also need to come back from time to time."

Deacon walked to a wet bar in the corner. "Can I get you something to drink?"

"Yes, please. I don't really care what it is, but make it a double."

She watched as Deacon poured them both a drink over ice and carried them over to the cof-fee table. Cecelia immediately picked up her glass and took a large sip. The amber liquid burned on the way down, distracting her from her nerves and eventually warming her blood. "I want to start by apologizing for that morning I ran out on you. I panicked and handled it poorly, and I haven't done any better since then."

Deacon didn't respond. He just sat patiently listening and taking the occasional sip of his own drink. She wasn't used to having someone's undivided attention, so she knew she needed to make the most of it.

"Everything in my life is falling apart," she said. "I don't know if you've been in town long enough to hear about Maverick, but he's been targeting members of the club since the beginning of the year. No one is sure who he is, or how he got the information, but he's been blackmailing people and spilling their secrets. I'm his latest victim."

That finally compelled Deacon to break his silence. "What could you have possibly done to be blackmailed for? Your parents always kept such a tight leash on you, I can't imagine you got into too much trouble over the years."

"He's not blackmailing me about something that I did. He's blackmailing me because of who I really am. Somehow Maverick has gotten a hold of my original birth certificate. He's threatening to tell everyone about my mother and her deadly drug habit. Up until now, no one has known the truth except for me, you and my parents."

Deacon frowned. "I don't see how anybody could

hold something like that against you. Why don't you just tell people the truth and take his power away?"

Cecelia sighed. "I thought about doing that, but my parents were very strongly against it. They don't want to ruin the image of the picture-perfect family they've created over the years. I paid the blackmailer, but he still went ahead and started sending out messages to club members that alluded to me. I got another one from him today demanding another payment. There's no way out of this trap. I tried to confide in Chip, thinking that he could help me somehow, but he accused me of living a lie and broke off our engagement instead."

When Cecelia turned to look at Deacon, his jaw was tight and his skin was flushed with anger. "What a bastard! I can't believe you were going to marry a man who could be so careless with your heart. You deserve better than him, Cecelia, not the other way around. By the time he figures that out, I hope it's too late for him to win you back."

Once again, she was stunned by his words. She just couldn't understand how he could say things like that to her after everything that she had done to him. "Why are you being so nice to me, Deacon? I don't deserve it."

Deacon reached out and took her hand in his. His warm touch sent a surge of awareness through her whole body, bringing back to mind memories of their recent night together. She pushed all of that aside and tried to focus on the here and now.

"What are you talking about? You've already apologized twice for the other night, unnecessarily I might add."

Cecelia met his gaze with her own. "I'm talking about high school. We were in love, we had made plans to run away and live this amazing life together, and I threw it all away. Don't you hate me for that?"

"I was angry for a while, but I have to admit that it fueled me to make more of myself. I couldn't hate you, Cecelia. I tried to, but I just couldn't. The girl I loved wasn't the one who broke up with me that day."

Cecelia felt a sense of relief wash over her. At least that was one thing she hadn't completely ruined. "I've never been strong enough, despite all my successes, to stand up to my parents. I made the mistake of telling them that after graduation, I was leaving with you. They had a fit and laid down the law. I wasn't going anywhere, they insisted. It broke my heart to break up with you, but I didn't know what else to do. And now, when they told me to keep my mouth shut and pay the blackmailer, I did it even though I didn't want to. I dated Chip for years because that's what they wanted. I probably would've married him to make them happy if he hadn't broken up with me. They've never really allowed me to be myself. I've always had to be this perfect daughter, striving to prove to them that I'm better than my mother was.

"I've only ever done two things in my life just because it made me happy. One was starting my business. Marriage and family didn't come as quickly as I'd hoped, so designing and decorating nurseries for a living was the next best thing."

Deacon stroked his thumb gently across the back of her hand as she spoke. "What was the other thing?"

She looked at him, a soft smile curling her lips. "Falling in love with you. You made me happy. You never asked me to be anybody other than who I was. You knew the truth about my mother, and it never seemed to bother you."

"That's because you were perfect just the way you were, Cecelia. Why would I ask you to change?"

No one had ever spoken to her the way Deacon did. His sincere words easily melted her defenses, cracking the cold businesswoman facade that she worked so hard to maintain. She'd always felt so alone, and she didn't want to be alone anymore.

Unwelcome tears started to well up in her eyes. Cecelia hated to cry, especially in front of other people. She wasn't raised to show that kind of vulnerability to anybody. In the Morgan household, she learned at a very young age that emotions made one appear weak, and that wasn't tolerated. Her birth mother had been weak, they'd told her, and look where she had ended up.

"I'm sorry," she said, pulling away from him to wipe her tears away.

"Stop apologizing," he said. He reached for her and pulled her into the protective cocoon of his strong embrace. Cecelia gave in to it, collapsing against him and letting her tears flow freely at last. He held her for what felt like an hour, although it was probably just a few minutes. When she was all out of tears, she sat up and looked at him.

Deacon's face was so familiar and yet so different after all these years. He still had the same kind eyes and charming smile she'd fallen in love with, there was just more maturity behind his gaze now. She found that wisdom made him more handsome than ever before.

In that moment, she didn't want him to just hold her. She wanted to surrender to him and offer him anything she had to give. Slowly, she leaned in and pressed her lips against his. This kiss was different from the one they'd shared before. There was no desperation or anger fueling it this time, just a swelling of emotion and her slow-burning desire for him.

Deacon didn't push her away, nor did he press

the kiss any further. It was firm and sweet, soft and tender, reminding her of warm summer nights spent lying in the back of his pickup truck. It was a kiss of potential, of promise.

Cecelia wanted more, but as she leaned farther into Deacon, she felt his hands press softly but insistently against her shoulders. When their lips parted, they sat together inches apart for a moment without speaking.

Finally Deacon said, "That's probably where we should end tonight. I don't want you to have any more regrets where I'm concerned. Or expectations."

Cecelia didn't regret a thing about what had happened between them, but she understood what he meant. What future could they possibly have together? She was still picking up the pieces from her broken engagement, and he'd be back in France in mere weeks. She nodded and sat back, feeling the chill rush in as the warmth of his body left her.

Setting her drink on the coffee table, Cecelia stood up. "I'd probably better get going, then. Thank you for listening and being so supportive. You don't know how rare that is in my life."

Deacon walked her to the door, giving her a firm but chaste hug before she left. It felt good just to be in his arms. She felt safe there, as though Maverick—and Chip and her parents and the gossipmongers of Royal—couldn't hurt her while Deacon was around.

"I'll see you at work tomorrow," he said.

Cecelia waved at him over her shoulder, feeling an unusual surge of optimism run through her as she climbed into her car. For the first time in a long time, she couldn't wait to see what life had in store for her.

Six

"The chef has put together the tasting menu for the grand opening celebration. I didn't realize it was happening today, and I promised Brandee that I would go with her to shop for some things for the ranch. Can you handle it without me?"

Deacon looked up from his desk and frowned at his business partner. "I may have lived in Europe for the last few years, but I don't exactly have the most refined tastes. I am a meat-and-potatoes kind of guy. Are you sure you want to leave the menu up to me? That's a pretty important element of the party, considering we're trying to lure customers into the new tapas restaurant."

"I wouldn't worry about it. We hired the best Spanish chef in all of Texas to run the restaurant. I'm pretty sure that anything Chef Eduardo makes is going to be amazing. If you're worried about it," Shane said with a wicked grin, "you could always ask Cecelia to join you. She's known for having excellent taste, in design and event planning."

Deacon sat back in his chair and considered Shane's suggestion. Since their kiss a few days ago, he had been considering his next move where she was concerned. He knew that he should back off before they both ended up in over their heads. The past had proven that his and Cecelia's relationship was doomed. They weren't the same people they were back in high school. Even so, he found his thoughts circling back to her again and again.

So what now? He wanted to spend some time with her. A date seemed too formal, especially since she might not want to be seen out with another man so soon after her engagement was called off. But this would be an interesting alternative if she had the time. "Okay, fine. You're off the hook. Get out of here and go buy some barbed wire or a horse or something."

Shane waved and disappeared down the hall. Deacon got up from his desk and went in search of Cecelia. He found her in the lobby directing the hanging of a large oil painting. It was a Western landscape, one of the few nods to Texas in her otherwise modern design.

"Perfect!" she declared after the level showed the frame was aligned just right.

"Well, thank you, I try," Deacon said from over her shoulder.

Cecelia spun on her heel and turned to look at him. "Very funny. Can I help you with something, Mr. Chase?"

Even now, always business first. Thankfully, he truly had a business proposition for her, even if his motivation was less than pure. "Actually, I was wondering if I could borrow you for an hour to help me with something."

"An hour? It's almost lunchtime."

"Which means…all your guys will be out in search of a taco truck and you will have nothing better to do than to join me for a private tasting at the new restaurant here in the hotel."

She arched an eyebrow at him, but she didn't say no. "Is the chef still working on the menu?"

"No, that's already set for both restaurants. What Chef Eduardo has put together for today is the menu for the grand opening gala. It features some of the items that will be on the restaurant's menu, but also some more finger-food-type selections that can be passed around by waiters. Shane was supposed to do this with me, but he's gotten roped into a shopping excursion with Brandee. That just leaves me, and I'm afraid I don't have the palate for this. I could use a second opinion."

Cecelia's gaze flicked over him for a moment, and then she nodded. She turned back to her crew. "Why don't you guys go ahead and take lunch? We'll finish up the rest of the paintings this afternoon."

She didn't have to tell them twice. The men immediately put down their tools and slipped out of the back of the hotel. Once they were gone, Cecelia turned back to Deacon with a smile. "Lead the way, Mr. Chase."

Technically, it wasn't a date, but Deacon felt inclined to offer her his arm and escort her down the hallway anyway. The Bellamy was designed with two dining options. The Silver Saddle was the more casual of the two, offering an upscale bar environment and featuring a selection of Spanish tapas in lieu of the typical appetizer selection. The other restaurant was the Glass House, a high-end farm-to-table restaurant, featuring all the freshest organic produce and responsibly sourced game available. The executive chef was even working on a rooftop garden where he intended to grow his own herbs and a selection of seasonable vegetables.

Normally, the Glass House would've been the appropriate venue for the grand opening, but Deacon had had other ideas. It wouldn't take much to lure the residents of Royal to the Glass House. That was right up their snooty, rich alley. Spanish tapas were another matter. Deacon had suggested that the food for the event be catered by the Silver Saddle instead, so they could introduce the town to what he and Shane hoped would be the newest hot spot in Royal.

When they arrived at the bar they found the executive chef waiting for them. Eduardo welcomed them with a wide smile. "Mr. Chase, I hope that you and your guest are very hungry."

"We are," Deacon replied. He'd seen a mock-up of the menu and knew they were in for a treat. He didn't actually expect to make many, if any, changes. Eduardo knew what he was doing. It was just good for him to know in advance what his guests had in store for them. "I can't wait to see what you put together."

Eduardo directed them to a corner booth. The decor of the bar was still a work in progress, but the majority of the key elements were in place. Along the edge of the room, the space was lined with burgundy leather booths and worn wooden tables. In the center was a rectangular bar that was accessible to guests on all sides. On the far side of the room from where they were seated, there was a stage for live music and a dance floor. Overhead, instead of a disco ball, Deacon had custom ordered a mirrored saddle, the bar's namesake.

They had gone for a cowboy atmosphere with a modern edge, much like Cecelia's room design, and Deacon was pretty sure they'd nailed it. In two months' time, he had no doubt that this place would be hopping on a Saturday night.

He helped Cecelia into the booth and then sat opposite of her. Before they could place their napkins in their laps, Eduardo called the first waiter to the table with a tray of four different beverages. He set them down and disappeared back into the kitchen.

"First, I wanted to start with the beverage selection for the evening. Of course we will have an open bar that will provide whatever beverages the guests would like. However, we will be showcasing the Silver Saddle's four featured drinks, as well." He pointed to the two wineglasses. "Here are our two signature sangrias. The first is a traditional red wine sangria, and this here is a strawberry rosé sangria.

"Next is our take on an Arnold Palmer, but instead of sweet tea, we use sweet-tea-flavored vodka and a sprig of rosemary in the lemonade. Last is the Viva Bellamy, designed exclusively for the hotel, with aged rye whiskey, sweet vermouth, blood-orange liqueur and orange bitters. Please enjoy, and we'll be out with the first round of tapas momentarily." Eduardo turned and disappeared into the kitchen.

"I have to say the best part of my job might be that I get to drink without ending up in the HR office," Deacon quipped with a grin as he picked up the old-fashioned glass containing the Viva Bellamy.

Cecelia opted for the rosé sangria. She took a sip and then smiled. "This is wonderful. It might be the best sangria I have ever had, actually. Try it."

She held the wineglass up to his lips and tipped it until the sweet concoction flowed into his mouth. It was a lovely beverage, but that wasn't what caught his attention. He was far more focused on Cecelia as she watched him. Perhaps Shane was smarter than Deacon gave him credit for. Feeding each other tapas could be quite the unexpectedly sensual experience for a weekday lunch at work.

Eduardo and the waiter returned a moment later with a selection of small plates. "Here we have stuffed piquillo peppers with goat cheese and seasonal mushrooms, seared scallops with English pea puree, chicken skewers with ajillo sauce, and black garlic and grilled lamb with rosemary sauce. Enjoy."

"Wow," Cecelia said. "This all looks amazing, and not at all what I was expecting from a place with a disco saddle hanging over the dance floor.

I'd wager there's no place like this within a hundred miles of here. People are going to trip over themselves to get to your restaurant, Deacon."

He certainly hoped so. The array of food was both heavenly scented and visually impressive. He could just picture it being passed around on silver platters and arranged artfully along a buffet display. "Shall we?" he asked.

Cecelia nodded and looked around, considering where to start. "Do we share everything? I've never done tapas before, but this kind of reminds me of dim sum."

"Yes, it's similar. *Tapas* means small plates, so it's just tiny selections of many different, shareable dishes instead of large entrée. Just try whatever you like."

She started by reaching out and pulling a chicken skewer onto one of the empty plates they'd each been given to make the tasting easier. Deacon opted for the lamb.

Cecelia closed her eyes and made a moaning sound of pure pleasure that Deacon recognized from their night together. His body stirred at the memory of that sound echoing in his bedroom.

"Wow," she said as she swallowed her bite and opened her eyes. "I mean, I know I said that already, but it's true, this is so good. You have to try it." She slid a piece of the chicken off the wooden skewer, stabbed it with her fork and held it out to him.

Deacon took a bite and chewed thoughtfully. The flavors were excellent. Her feeding him wasn't bad, either, but he would much prefer to feed her. "That's good. Do you like lamb?"

She nodded. He took the opportunity to stab a small cube of lamb and feed it to her. She closed her eyes again as she chewed, thoroughly enjoying the food in a way he hadn't expected. She'd become quite the foodie since the last time they were together. He suddenly lost interest in trying the food himself, and wanted only to feed Cecelia.

He picked up one of the small stuffed peppers with his fingers and held it up to her. She leaned in, looking into his eyes as she took a bite. Her lips softly brushed his fingertips, sending a shiver through his whole body. When she finished, she took the second bite from his fingers. He tried to pull his hand away but she grabbed his wrist and held it steady.

"Don't you dare waste that sauce," she said. Without hesitation she drew his thumb into her mouth and sucked the spicy cream sauce from his skin.

Deacon almost came up out of his seat. The suction on this thumb combined with the swirl of her tongue against his skin made every muscle in his body tense up and his blood rush to his groin. She seemed unaffected. Cecelia pulled away with a sly smile, releasing his wrist. As though she hadn't just given him oral pleasure, albeit to his hand, she turned back to the selection on the table and chose one of the scallops.

She was just messing with him now. And he liked it.

The plates just kept coming out of the kitchen, and Cecelia found herself in food heaven. Her roommate in college had been the daughter of a famous Manhattan chef, and she'd exposed Cecelia to cuisines she hadn't tried back home in Texas. She'd developed a brave palate and high expectations by the time she'd graduated. The little diner in Royal had been fine before she left, but when she returned, she found herself trekking to Houston for cuisine with more flair and spice.

Now she'd have access to world-class dining right here in Royal. At that moment, Eduardo and his waiter brought out fried chorizo wrapped in thin slices of potato, a selection of imported jamón ibérico and Spanish cheeses, marinated and grilled vegetables in a Romanesco sauce, garlic shrimp and salmon tartare in salmon roe cones. By the time they got to the dessert selections, Cecelia wasn't sure she could eat much more. She loved her sweets, but she was far more interested in the tall, handsome dish across from her at the moment.

Cecelia would be lying if she said that she hadn't been thinking about Deacon since they shared that kiss Monday night. Part of her wondered if that had been his plan all along—to kiss her, send her home and leave her wanting more.

Cecelia did want more. There was no question of it. She just wasn't sure if indulging her desires was the best idea. There was certainly plenty of sexual attraction flowing between them, and their night of passion would be one she would never forget. But could she risk giving herself to Deacon when she knew she might fall for him again?

It happened so quickly the first time, Cecelia had hardly known what hit her. For a while after they'd broken up, she had thought that perhaps falling in love was easy to do. The years that followed would prove otherwise. No one, not even her ex-fiancé, had captured her heart the way Deacon had. She feared he still had that power over her.

The hotel opened in a little more than two weeks. Deacon had told her that once things were up and running, he would return to Cannes. She couldn't risk his taking her heart with him when he left. A few weeks didn't seem like much time to be together, but Deacon was a well-known commodity to Cecelia. She knew the kind soul she once loved was still there, so even that short time was enough for her to fall miserably in love with him again, just to have him disappear from her life like before.

Cecelia wouldn't let herself believe that this was a second chance to put things right between them. They could make peace, and already had, really, but a relationship between them seemed impossible. Even if he weren't returning to the French Riviera in a few weeks, they both knew she was in no position to start something promising with anyone. Not with Maverick's threat hanging overhead.

She wouldn't blame him for indulging while he was here and not getting attached. Hell, if *he* broke *her* heart this time, it would be some sort of karmic retribution somehow. She deserved it.

Maybe she was just a masochist, but she couldn't walk away from him. Not twice in a lifetime.

"I've got to sample dessert," Deacon said, oblivious to her train of thought. "I might explode or spend this afternoon napping in my office, but I told Shane that I would try everything." He eyed the selection of desserts on the table with dismay.

"I think you've still got room," she said. She reached out and picked up a berry tartlet, bringing it up to his lips. "Take a bite."

He didn't resist. Deacon bit down into the sweet treat, taking half of it into his mouth. Chewing, he watched as she brought the rest of it up to her mouth and finished it off with a satisfied sound.

"Yummy," she said and picked up another treat. This one was a small brownie with whipped cream and a dusting of what looked like chili powder. That would be interesting.

As they made their way through the rest of the desserts, Cecelia could feel them building toward something more. If it wasn't the middle of the afternoon, she was certain he would take her home and make love to her. As it was, she wouldn't be surprised if he escorted her into his office and locked the door. The entire meal had been the tastiest foreplay she'd ever had. It made her want to spend the weekend in bed with him, and she would if it wasn't for that pesky engagement party she had to go to tomorrow night.

It occurred to her that there might be one way to get through the evening after all. "Deacon, can I ask you for a favor?"

He leaned in, causing the most delicious tingles as he smoothed his palm down her arm. "Anything."

"Would you go with me to Wes and Isabelle's engagement party at the club?" She had no doubt that the gossip would be flying about her breakup with Chip, and it would be so much easier if she had Deacon there with her to soften the blow.

Deacon narrowed his gaze at her. "The club? The Texas Cattleman's Club? Are you serious?"

Cecelia frowned. "Of course I'm serious. Why wouldn't I be serious? I'm a member. Everyone in town practically is a member now. What's the big deal?"

With a sigh, Deacon sat back against the leather of the booth. "The big deal is that I'm not a member. They would never *let* me be a member. I don't exactly relish hanging out someplace where I'm not wanted."

Sometimes Cecelia forgot how hard it was for Deacon to live in Royal back when they were kids. He had never fit in with the others driving the BMWs they got for their sweet sixteenth and going home to their mansions at night. She never really thought about it, because none of it ever mattered to her. He had simply been the most wonderful boy she'd ever known. The fact that he'd driven a beat-up pickup truck and lived in a small, unimpressive house on the edge of town hadn't been important.

But it had been important to him both then and now, gauging by his reaction. Even though he was successful, even though he could buy and sell half the people in this town, he still had a chip on his shoulder.

"You're not seventeen and broke anymore, Deacon. Stop worrying about all those other people and what they might or might not think. Actually, most of them are so self-centered that they won't be nearly as concerned with your being at the club as they will be about a million other things."

She leaned into him and took his hand. The touch of his skin against hers made her long for the night they'd spent together with his hands gliding over her naked body. Cecelia really did want him to go to the party with her, and not just as a buffer from the ire of the town. She wanted to go back to his place afterward and spend all night relishing the feel of him against her.

Cecelia looked in his eyes, hoping they reflected her intentions and thoughts. She stroked the back of his hand with her thumb in the slow, lazy circles guaranteed to drive him wild and get her exactly what she wanted. "Come with me. Please."

Jaw tight, his gaze dropped to his hand. With a soft shake of his head, he sighed. "Okay, you win. When is this engagement party?"

"Tomorrow night. Seven o'clock. Will that work for you?"

Deacon nodded. "I suppose. Will I get some sort of special reward for being your escort for the evening?" he asked with a grin lighting his eyes.

"You absolutely will," she promised. "Do you have anything in mind?"

"I do." Deacon took her hand and scooped it up

in his own. He pressed his fingertips into the palm of her hand and stroked gently but firmly, turning her own trick on her. It was easy to imagine those hands on her body, those fingers stroking the fires that burned deep inside her. "What are you doing after work today?" he asked.

Her gaze met his, a small smile curling her lips even as he continued to tease her with his fingertips. "Nothing much," she said coyly. "What do you plan to do tonight?"

Deacon leaned into her, burying his fingers in the loose hair at the nape of her neck and bringing her lips a fraction of an inch from his own. She wanted to close the gap between them and lose herself in his kiss. It was all she wanted, all she could think of when they were this close. She could feel the warmth of his breath on her lips. Her tongue snaked across her bottom lip to wet it in anticipation of his kiss.

Instead he smiled and let his fingers trace along the line of her jaw. "Why, I plan to be doing *you*, Miss Morgan."

YOUR PARTICIPATION IS REQUESTED!

Dear Reader,

Since you are a lover of our books – we would like to get to know you!

Inside you will find a short Reader's Survey. Sharing your answers with us will help our editorial staff understand who you are and what activities you enjoy.

To thank you for your participation, we would like to send you 2 books and 2 gifts – **ABSOLUTELY FREE!**

Enjoy your gifts with our appreciation,

Pam Powers

SEE INSIDE FOR READER'S SURVEY

For Your Reading Pleasure...

We'll send you 2 books and 2 gifts
ABSOLUTELY FREE
just for completing our Reader's Survey!

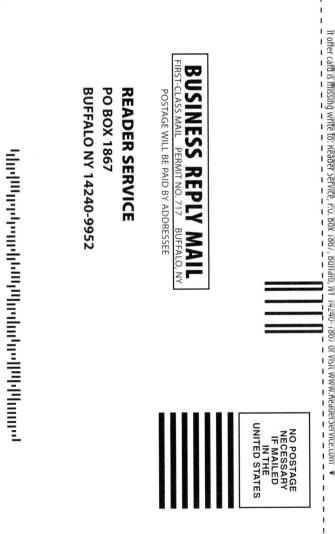

Seven

"So, are you friends with Wes or Isabelle?" Deacon asked as they slipped into the crowd mingling at the clubhouse.

Cecelia twisted her lips as she tried to come up with a good answer. "Neither, really. Wes and I are business rivals. We dated a while back, but that's it. I don't really know Isabelle that well, either."

"Why would he invite his ex to his engagement party?"

That was a good question, considering she was also the reason he'd gone years without knowing he had a daughter. She still felt bad about misjudging that whole situation. She'd helped to correct it in the end, but Wes would never get that time back, and that was her fault. "Well, in a roundabout way, I did help bring him and Isabelle back together after they broke up a few years ago."

"How's that?"

She shook her head and reached out for a flute of champagne being passed on a tray by a waiter in the standard black-and-white uniform of the club. Cecelia hesitated to tell Deacon what she'd done. He still saw her as the sweet girl he'd dated in school, and she didn't want him to see her any differently. "You don't want to know."

"Not good?" Deacon asked.

She shrugged. "Let's just say it wasn't my finest moment. But it all turned out well in the end, and since Isabelle invited me despite it all, I knew I needed to come and work on mending those bridges." Leaning into him, she spoke quieter so others nearby couldn't hear her. "I fear that before too long, I'll need all the friends I can get."

Deacon slipped a protective arm around her waist. "If anyone so much as says an ugly word to you tonight, I'll punch them in the jaw."

Cecelia smiled and leaned into his embrace. She wouldn't mind seeing Chip sprawled across the worn hardwood floor of the club, but that would cause more trouble than it was worth. And she probably deserved some of those ugly words. "That won't be necessary, but thank you."

As they turned back toward the crowd, the people parted and Isabelle rushed forward to give Cecelia a hug. She looked radiant tonight in a shimmering bronze cocktail dress that brought out the copper in her hazel eyes. "Cecelia, you made it! I'm so glad."

Cecelia accepted the hug and smiled as warmly as she could. Once she realized she'd been wrong about Isabelle's gold-digging ways, she found she really did like her. Now she just had to fight off the pangs of envy where Wes's fiancée was concerned. Soon, Isabelle would have the family that Cecelia had always wanted. She shouldn't hold that against her, though. It was a long time coming, raising Caroline as a single mother, in part because of Cecelia's meddling.

Turning to her date, Cecelia introduced them. "Isabelle, this is Deacon Chase. He's building The Bellamy with Shane Delgado."

Isabelle smiled and shook his hand. "I'm so excited for the hotel to open. It looks amazing from the outside."

Cecelia could tell Deacon was nervous, but he was handling it well. "Thank you," he said politely. "It looks amazing on the inside, too, thanks to Cecelia's great designs. Congratulations on your engagement."

"Thank you."

"It looks like a great turnout," Cecelia noted. "Even Teddy Bradford is here." That was a surprise to everyone, she was certain. She knew the CEO of Playco had been in merger negotiations with Wes before Maverick outed him as a deadbeat dad. Teddy espoused family values and had dropped Wes's Texas Toy Company like a rock when he found out about Isabelle and Caroline.

"I actually invited him," Isabelle confided. "I haven't given up on the Playco merger, even if Wes thinks all is lost. I'm hoping that when he sees us together he'll reconsider the deal."

Cecelia could only nod blankly at Isabelle's machinations. The merger of Playco and Texas Toy Company wouldn't be good news for To the Moon and its bottom line, which is why Cecelia had kept her mouth shut where that was concerned. Wes was her biggest business rival. However, the success of Luna Fine Furnishings would make her untouchable if she could compete in both the adult and child luxury design markets. At the moment, things were going well enough that she didn't care if Teddy took Wes back.

"Good luck with that," she managed politely. "And congratulations on the engagement."

Isabelle crossed her fingers and said her good-byes, slipping away to find Wes in the crowd. Once she was gone, Cecelia and Deacon continued to make their way through the room, saying hello and mingling appropriately. When they found the food, they each made a small plate and had a seat among some of the other guests. A long buffet had been set up for the party, with the centerpiece being a cake shaped like two hearts side by side with a third, smaller heart piped in pastel pink icing on top to represent their daughter. It was sweet.

They were perhaps an hour into the party, with no sign of Chip, and Cecelia was finally starting to relax. Maybe this event wouldn't be such a night-mare. Being there with Deacon had changed everything. She felt confident on his arm, which was a far cry from the times she'd gone to events with Chip. She was always on edge with him, wondering if she looked good enough, if she was saying the right thing... Now that it was over, she couldn't imagine a lifetime of being his wife. All she would have ever been was a prop he'd haul out at campaign rallies and fund-raisers. A Stepford wife in a tasteful linen suit with helmet hair and a single strand of pearls.

No way. Those days were behind her, and she'd never make that mistake again.

"I would like to propose a toast," Teddy Bradford said as he took position center stage with the microphone to draw everyone's attention. Cecelia noted that the boisterous old man was wearing his best bolo tie for the occasion. The crowd gathered around the stage to hear what he had to say. "Wesley, Isabelle, get on up here!"

The happy couple walked hand in hand to the stage and to stand beside Teddy.

"No one here is happier to see these two lovebirds tie the knot than I am. To me, and to the employees of Playco, family is everything. I had thought that perhaps Wesley felt differently, but I'm pleased—for once—to be proven wrong. Not only do I want to wish the couple all the happiness in the world, I want to wish it as Wesley's new business partner."

His words were followed by a roar of applause from the crowd. Wes turned to Isabelle with a look of shock on his face before he turned and shook Teddy's hand. Cecelia could only smile. Isabelle seemed sweet, but she was shrewd, as well. She had managed to accomplish tonight what Wes had been unable to over the past three months. Bravo. Perhaps she had more competition in the Texas Toy Company than she thought with Isabelle behind the scenes.

Wes turned back to Isabelle, they kissed and everyone in the club went wild. Deacon held Cecelia tighter to his side as though he sensed tension in her.

"Is this bad news for your company?" he whispered in her ear. Clearly, he knew it was or he wouldn't be asking.

"Perhaps, but I'm trying not to look at it that way. Those kinds of thoughts were what landed me such a miserable reputation in town. That's a worry for another day. Tonight I'd rather focus on the happy couple."

He nodded and pressed a kiss into her temple. "Then that's what we're going to do."

Cecelia sighed contentedly in his arms while Isabelle and Wes cut the cake and pieces started circulating around the room. "They cut the cake," she noted. "Cake is the universal sign at parties that it's finally okay to take your leave."

"Are you ready to go so soon?" Deacon asked. "I thought you were having a good time. And it looks like strawberry cake. We should probably at least stick around to have some. I love strawberry cake."

"When did you get such a sweet tooth?" Cecelia asked.

"It started back in high school when I couldn't get enough of your sugar."

Cecelia laughed aloud and leaned close. "You don't need any cake, then. You're getting plenty of sugar once we get out of here. You've made it through the night with no complaints, and you should be rewarded."

Deacon smiled. "I'm glad you agree. It wasn't that bad, though." His glance moved around the room at the club and the people who frequented it. "I think I'd made more of this place in my mind because I couldn't be a part of it."

"No one would dare keep you out now."

Cecelia felt her phone vibrate in her purse, but she wasn't going to get it out just yet. As they waited on cake, she noticed quite a few people pulling theirs out.

"Oh, my God, honey." Simone ran up to her and clapped her hand over her mouth to hold back a sob.

Cecelia looked at her and again around the room in sudden panic. One person after another seemed to be looking down at his or her phone. The feeling of dread was hard for Cecelia to suppress. Especially when those same people immediately sought out Cecelia when they looked up.

Had Maverick's deadline already come and gone so soon? She had consciously decided not to pay the blackmail money again, but she never dreamed it would come out tonight, while she was at the club with everyone else.

"What is it?" she asked as innocently as she could, although she already knew the answer.

Simone held up her phone, showing the screen

to her and Deacon. An old newspaper article about the drug overdose of Nicole Wood was there. It even featured the photo of Nicole and her infant daughter, the same one Cecelia carried in her purse. The section was circled in red and accompanied by a note:

Cecelia Morgan? More like Cecelia Wood—a liar and the daughter of a junkie and her dealer. No wonder the Morgans hid the truth. The homecoming queen isn't so perfect now, is she?

Deacon's arms tightened around Cecelia as she felt her knees start to buckle beneath her. It was only his support that kept her upright. She looked around the room, and it seemed like everyone was looking at her as though she smelled like horse manure.

Her head started to swim as she heard the voices in the room combine together into a low rumble. She could pick out only pieces of it.

"Who knew she was so low class?"

"I should've known she wasn't really a Morgan. But it looks like she's not Maverick, either."

"Her mother probably used drugs during her pregnancy, too. I wonder if that's why Cecelia is so incapable of empathy."

"Have they ever revoked someone's club membership for fraud?"

"You can see the resemblance between her and this Nicole woman. She never had Tilly's classically beautiful features."

Cecelia covered her ears with her hands to smother the voices. Her face flushed red, and tears started pouring from her eyes. Deacon said something to her, but she couldn't hear him. All she could feel was her world crumbling around her. She should've made the second blackmail payment. What was she thinking? That he would decide maybe that first payment was enough? That people wouldn't judge her the way she would've judged them not long ago?

It was a huge mistake, and yet, she knew this was a moment that couldn't be avoided no matter how much cash she shelled out. It wasn't about the money, she knew that much. He probably didn't care if he made a dime in the process. Maverick was set on ruining people's lives.

He would be a happy man tonight.

Deacon didn't know who Maverick was, but he sure as hell was going to find out. Why did this sick bastard get pleasure out of hurting people in the club? Deacon would be the first to admit this wasn't his favorite crowd of people, but who would stoop that low? If he could get his hands on Maverick right now, the coward would have bigger concerns than whose life he could make miserable next.

First things first, however. He could see Cecelia breaking down, and it made his chest ache. He had to get her away from this. With every eye in the room on them, he wrapped his arm around Cecelia and tried to guide her to the exit. She stumbled a few times, as though her legs were useless beneath her, so he stopped long enough to scoop her into his arms and carry her out. She didn't fight his heroics. Instead, she clung desperately to him, burying her face in the lapel of his suit.

The crowd parted as they made their way to the door. Half the people in the room looked disgusted. Some were in shock. A few more looked worried, probably concerned that their dark secret might be the next exposed by Maverick. There were only a few people in the room who looked at all concerned about Cecelia herself, and that made him almost as angry as he was with the blackmailing bastard that started this mess.

That was the problem with this town—the cliquish bullshit was ridiculous. It was just as bad in high school as it was now. It made him glad that he'd decided to leave Royal instead of staying in this toxic environment.

The problem was that most of the people in

the town were in the clique, so they didn't see the issue. It was only the outsiders who suffered by their viper-pit mentality. Deacon had always been an outsider, and money and prestige hadn't changed that, not really. He'd gotten through the doors of the club tonight, but he still didn't fit in. And he didn't want to.

Yet if he had to bet money on Maverick's identity, he'd put it on another outsider. Whoever it was was just kicking the hornet's nest for fun, watching TCC members turn on each other so they would know what it felt like to be him.

Cecelia didn't need to be around for the fallout. This entire situation was out of her control, and she would be the one to suffer unnecessarily for it. Brent and Tilly should be here, taking on their share of the club's disgust for forcing her to live this lie to begin with. If they'd been honest about adopting Cecelia, there would've been nothing for Maverick to hold over her head.

He shoved the heavy oak door open with his foot and carried her out to the end of the portico. There, he settled her back on her feet. "Are you okay to stand?" he asked.

"Yes," she said, sniffing and wiping the streams of mascara from her flush cheeks.

"I'm going to go get my car. Will you be okay?"

She nodded. Deacon reached into his pocket to

get his keys, but before he could step into the parking lot, a figure stumbled out of the dark bushes nearby. He didn't recognize the man, but he didn't like the looks of him, either. He was thin with stringy hair and bugged-out eyes. Even without the stink of alcohol and the stumble in his steps, Deacon could tell this was a guy on the edge. Maybe even the kind of guy who would blackmail the whole town.

"Cecelia *Wood*?" he asked, with a lopsided smile that revealed a mess of teeth inside. "Shoulda seen that one coming, right? Nobody is that perfect. Even a princess like you needs to be knocked off their high horse every now and then, right?"

Deacon stepped protectively between him and Cecelia. "Who the hell is this guy?" he asked.

"Adam Haskell," she whispered over his shoulder. "He has a small ranch on the edge of town. I'm surprised he hasn't lost it to the banks yet. All he does is drink anymore."

The name sounded familiar from Deacon's childhood, but the man in front of him had lived too many rough years to be recognizable. "Why don't you call a cab and sleep that booze off, Adam?"

The drunk didn't even seem to hear him. He was focused entirely on Cecelia. "You had it coming, you know. You can only go through life treating people like dirt for so long before karma comes back and slaps you across the face. Now you're getting a taste of your own medicine."

"Now, that's enough," Deacon said more forcefully. This time he got Adam's attention.

"Look at Deacon Chase all grow-w-wn up," he slurred. "You should hate her as much as I do. She treated you worse than anyone else. Used you and spit you out when she didn't need you anymore."

"Adam!" A man's sharp voice came from the doorway of the club. A lanky but solid man with short blond hair stepped outside with a redhead at his side.

"Mac and Violet McCallum!" Adam said as he turned his attention to them, nearly losing his drunken footing and falling over. "You're just in time. I was telling Deacon here how he's made a mistake trying to protect her. She's made her bed, it's time for her to lie in it, don't you think?"

Deacon's hands curled into fists of rage at his sides. He was getting tired of this guy's mouth. If he couldn't get his hands on Maverick, Mr. Haskell would do in a pinch.

"All right, Adam, you know you're not supposed to be here on the property if you're not a member of the club. They'll call the sheriff on you again. You can't afford the bail."

"Best sleep I ever get is in the drunk tank," he declared proudly, then belched.

"Even then." Mac came up to Adam and put an arm around his shoulder. "How about we give you a ride home, Adam? You don't need to be driving."

Adam pouted in disappointment, but he didn't fight Mac off. "Aw, I'm just having a little fun with her. Right, Cecelia? No harm done."

Mac just shook his head. "Well, tonight's not a good night for it. I'm pretty sure the party is over. If you stay around here any longer, it might be a fist and not the vodka that knocks you out tonight."

Mac was right. Deacon was glad the couple had intervened when they had or he might've had to get physical with the scrawny drunk.

"I can take anyone," Adam muttered.

"I'm sure you can," Mac agreed and rolled his eyes. "But let's not risk it tonight and ruin Isabelle's party any more than it already has been."

Mac led Adam toward his truck while Violet stayed behind with Deacon and Cecelia. "I'm so sorry, Cecelia," she said. "This whole thing with Maverick is getting out of hand. I can't imagine who would want to hurt everyone so badly. And the way people reacted…it's not right."

Cecelia came out from behind Deacon, still clinging to his arm. "Thank you, Violet."

The redhead just nodded sadly and followed Mac and Adam out into the parking lot. Cecelia watched her go with a heavy sigh. "There goes one of the five people in town who hasn't turned on me."

He hated hearing that kind of defeat from her. Cecelia was his fighter. He wasn't about to let Maverick beat her down. "You know what you need?" Deacon asked. "You need to get away from here."

She nodded. "Yeah, I'd like to go home if you don't mind."

Home wouldn't help. Word about her would just spread through town like wildfire, and soon everyone would know. Her parents would show up lamenting how embarrassing this was for them and making Cecelia feel even worse. Her friends would drop in to commiserate and reopen the wounds she was struggling to heal. No, she needed to get the hell out of Royal for a few days.

"I have another idea." Deacon took her hand and led her to his car. After the scene with Adam, he was too worried to leave her alone in case a partygoer came out of the club and had something nasty to say. When they got to his car, he opened the door and helped her in. "You're not going home."

She looked at him in surprise. "I'm not? Where are we going, then? To your place?"

Deacon shook his head and closed her door. He climbed into his side and revved the engine. He had bigger, better plans than just hiding her away at his wood-and-stone sanctuary. "I guess you could look at it that way."

He pulled out of the parking lot and picked up his phone. He dialed his private jet service and made all the necessary arrangements while Cecelia sat looking confused and beat down in the seat beside him.

Finally, he hung up and put the phone down. "It's all handled."

Cecelia turned in her seat to look at him. "You said we were going to your place, but that's back the other way. Then you have some vague conversation about going home for a few days. That doesn't make any sense. Where are we going, Deacon?"

He smiled, hoping this little mystery was enough to distract her from the miserable night. "Well, first we're stopping at your place so you can pack a bag and grab your passport."

He turned in time to see her silvery, gray eyes widen. "My passport? Why on earth…?"

Deacon grinned. This was a turn of events he hadn't expected, but it was the perfect escape. She needed to get away, he wanted to show her his crown jewel…it all worked out. By the time they returned to Royal, perhaps some new gossip from Maverick would crop up and make everyone forget about Cecelia's birth mother.

"Yes, and once you're packed, we're going to the airport where a private jet is waiting to take the two of us to one of my other properties, the Hotel de Rêve."

Cecelia sat in shock beside him. It took a few moments before she could respond. "Deacon, your other hotel is in *France*."

He pulled into her driveway and put the Corvette into Park. "Yes. Hence the need for your passport. Pack for the French Riviera in the spring."

She shook her head, making her blond waves dance around her shoulders. Cecelia had really looked lovely tonight, in a beautiful and clingy gray lace dress that brought out the gray in her eyes, but he'd barely had time to appreciate it between the mingling and the drama.

"No, Deacon, this is crazy talk. I can't go to France tonight even if I wanted to. The Bellamy opens in two weeks. I have so much to do—"

"*Your staff* has things to do," he interrupted, "and they know what those things are. You're not carrying furniture and wiring lamps into the wall. You're the designer, and most of your work is handled. Shane will oversee everything else, I promise. You and I are getting out of this town for a few days to let this whole mess blow over. End of discussion."

The way Cecelia looked at him, he could tell it wasn't the end of the discussion yet. "Couldn't we just go to Houston or something to get away? Maybe New Orleans? No one would know where we were. We don't have to go all the way to France, do we?"

Deacon disagreed. He turned off the car and got out, opening her door. "Yes, we do."

"Why?" she persisted as she stood to look at him.

"Because I don't own a hotel in New Orleans. Now get inside and pack that bag. The plane leaves for Cannes in an hour."

Eight

Cecelia woke up in a nest of soft, luxury linens with bright light streaming through the panoramic hotel room windows. Wincing from the light, she pushed herself up in bed and looked around the suite for Deacon. She could see him on the balcony reading a newspaper and drinking his café au lait at a tiny bistro table there.

She wrapped the blanket around her naked body and padded barefoot to the sliding glass door. The view from the owner's suite of the Hotel de Rêve was spectacular. The hotel was almost directly on the beach, with only the famous Boulevard de la

Croisette separating his property from the golden sands that lined the Mediterranean Sea. To the left of the hotel was a marina filled with some the largest and most luxurious yachts she'd ever seen. To the right, beautiful, tan tourists had already taken up residence on the beach.

The sea was a deep turquoise against the bright robin's-egg blue of the sky. There wasn't a cloud, a blemish, a single thing to ruin the perfection. It was almost as if the place wasn't real. When they'd first arrived the day before, Cecelia wasn't entirely certain that this wasn't a delusion brought on by jet lag. But after a quick nap, Cannes was just as pretty as it had been earlier. Of course, enjoying it with the handsome—and partially clothed—hotel owner hadn't hurt, either.

"*Bonjour, belle,*" he greeted her. He was sitting in a pair of black silk pajama pants, and thankfully, he seemed to have misplaced the top. His golden tan and chiseled chest and arms were on display, and now she knew how he had gotten that dark. If she spent every morning enjoying the sun here, she might actually get a little color for her porcelain complexion, as well.

Cecelia didn't know why she was surprised to find that he was fluent in French, considering Deacon had lived here for several years and had to interact with guests, locals and staff, alike. She supposed it just didn't align with the Deacon she had once known—covered in motor oil or rinsing cafeteria trays—although it suited Deacon perfectly as he was now.

It made her wish she had kept up with her French studies after high school. She'd quickly lost most of her vocabulary and conjugation, really being able to function now only as a tourist asking for directions to the nearest restroom. "*Bonjour*," she replied in her most practiced accent. "That's about all the French I have for today."

Deacon laughed and folded his paper, which was also in French. "That's okay," he said, leaning forward to give her a good-morning kiss. "Perhaps later we can crawl back into bed and practice a little more French."

Cecelia couldn't suppress the girlish giggle at his innuendo. Deacon was smart to bring her to Cannes. There was just something about being here, thousands of miles away from Royal and all her worries, that made her feel like a completely different person. She liked this person a hell of a lot more than the woman who had very nearly married Chip Ashford. Apparently most of Royal hadn't liked her, either, judging by their reaction to her being knocked down a peg or two by Maverick's gossip.

Cecelia sat down at the table next to him, and he poured her a cup of coffee, passing her the pitcher of milk to add as much as she would like. He followed it with a plate of flaky, fresh croissants and preserves.

"Do you have anything in mind that you would like to do today?" he asked. "Yesterday we were too exhausted to do much more than change time zones, but I thought you might like to see a little bit of the town this afternoon. You haven't been to Cannes if you haven't strolled along la Croisette, sipped a beautiful rosé and watched the sunset. We could even take my yacht out for a spin."

She took a large sip of her coffee and nodded into her delicate china teacup. "That sounds lovely. I've never been to the French Riviera, so I would be happy to see anything that you would like to show me. I mean," she continued, "it's not like this is a trip that I've planned for a long time. I basically just let you sweep me off my feet and I woke up in France. I would be perfectly content to just sit on this balcony and look out at the sea if that was all we had time to do."

Deacon smiled. "Well, I figure there is no place on earth better suited to relax and forget about all your problems than the French Riviera. I've seen more than one tightly wound businessman completely transform in only a few days. After everything that has happened recently, I think it's just what the doctor ordered, Miss Morgan."

She couldn't argue with that. He was absolutely right. Here, the drama of Maverick and the fallout of her exposed secret felt like a distant memory, or a dream that she'd nearly forgotten about as she'd awakened. She had gotten a couple texts from Simone and her mother yesterday morning after they'd landed, but Deacon had insisted she turn off her phone. Overage charges for international roaming were a good excuse, he'd said, and once again he had been right. She didn't want talk to her mother or anyone else right now.

She just wanted to soak in the glorious rays of the sun, enjoy the beauty around her and relish her time alone with Deacon. They would return home soon enough to open the hotel, and she'd finally face everything she had been running from her whole life.

"I took the liberty of scheduling an appointment for you at our spa today. My talented ladies have been told to give you the works, so a massage, a mud bath, a facial… Whatever your little heart desires. That should take up a good chunk of your day, and then we can hit the shore later this afternoon, once you've been properly pampered."

Cecelia could only shake her head and thank her lucky stars that she had Deacon here with her through all of this. How would she have coped alone? Just having him by her side would've been enough, but he always had to go the extra mile, and she appreciated it. She just wasn't sure how she could ever repay him.

She idly slathered a bit of orange marmalade on a piece of croissant and popped it into her mouth. "You're too good to me, Deacon," she said as she chewed thoughtfully. "I don't deserve any of this VIP treatment. I'm beginning to think that maybe Adam Haskell was right, and all the negativity I've been breeding all these years was just coming back to haunt me. It had to eventually, right?"

"You're too hard on yourself," Deacon said. "The girl I fell in love with was sweet and caring and saw things in me that no one else saw. You might pretend now that you are a cold-as-ice businesswoman set to crush your competitors and anybody who gets in your way, but I don't believe it for a second. That girl I know is still in there somewhere."

Cecelia appreciated that he had so much faith in her, but she wasn't the innocent girl he knew from back in school. That girl had been smothered the day her parents forced her to break up with Deacon and put her life back on track to the future that they wanted for her. She had become an unfortunate mix of both her parents—a cutthroat business owner, a perfection-seeking elitist and, more often than she would have liked, a plain old bitch. He hadn't been around to see the changes in her, but she knew it was true. She was absolutely certain that most of the people in town were thrilled to see her taken down a notch. Maybe even a few of the people whom she'd once considered her friends.

"I'm glad you think so highly of me, Deacon, but I can't help but wonder if you're actually seeing me as I am, or as you want to see me."

"I see you as you are, beneath the designer clothes, fancy makeup and social facade you've crafted. That girl hasn't changed. She's still in there, you just haven't let her out in a long time."

Cecelia felt tears start to well in her eyes as her cheeks burned with emotion. She really hoped that he was right, and that the good person he remembered was still here. It seemed like over the past decade she had lost touch with herself, if she had ever really known who she truly was. She'd spent her whole life trying to live up to her parents' expectations, then Chip's expectations…

Who *was* Cecelia Morgan anyway?

She wiped her damp cheek with the back of her hand and reached for her coffee cup to give her something to focus on instead of the emotions raging just beneath the surface. "I don't know who I am anymore."

Deacon leaned forward, resting his elbows on the knees of his pajama pants. "That's the beauty of being in charge of your own life and not trying to live up to anybody else's standards. You can do whatever you want to do. If I had just sat back and accepted the life that everyone expected of me, we wouldn't be sitting on the balcony of my five-star hotel in France. I wanted to be more, so I made myself more. You can be whoever you want to be, Cecelia, and if that means putting aside the mean-girl persona you've had all these years, and being the girl I used to know, you can do that, too."

"Can I?" she asked. "I'm not entirely sure that girl knew who she was, either. I was so easily manipulated at that age. I mean, all those plans we made, all those dreams we had for the future…that was important to me and I threw it all away. For what? Because my parents threatened to cut me off and throw me out of the house if I didn't."

Deacon's head turned sharply toward her. "What?"

Cecelia winced. "You didn't know that?"

His expression softened. "I suppose I knew they were ultimately behind your change of heart, but I thought you just wanted to please them as you always did."

"I did want to please them, but not about this. I loved you, Deacon. I didn't want to break up with you. It broke my heart to do it, but I felt like I didn't have any choice. They were my parents. The only people in the world who had wanted me when no one else did. I couldn't bear for them to turn their backs on me."

"I wanted you."

Cecelia looked into Deacon's serious green eyes and realized she had made a monumental mistake that day all those years ago. Yes, she had a booming business and he had been successful on his own, but what could they have built together? They'd never know.

"I was a fool," she admitted. "I don't want to make the same mistake again. I want to make the right choice for my life this time."

Cecelia sipped her coffee and tried to think of who she wanted to be. Not who her parents wanted her to be. Not who Chip expected her to be. The answer came to her faster than she anticipated. She wanted to be the woman she was when she was with Deacon. When she was with him she felt strong and brave and beautiful. She never felt like she wasn't good enough. That was how she wanted to feel: loved.

But could she feel that way without him? Their time together had been exciting and romantic, but she had no doubt there was a time limit. Deacon had no interest in staying in Royal. He didn't like the town and he didn't like the people, and for a good reason. When The Bellamy was opened and running, he would return here to France, and she didn't blame him. This may very well be the most beautiful place she'd ever seen. She would be eager to return, as well.

She might feel like a superhero when she was with him, but once she was alone, could she be her own kryptonite?

"Dinner was wonderful," Cecelia said.

Deacon took her hand and they strolled along la Croisette together. The sun had already set, leaving the sky a golden color that was quickly being overtaken by the inky purple of early evening. The lights from the shops and restaurants along the walkway lighted their path and the crests of the ocean waves beyond them.

"I'm glad you enjoyed it. There's no such thing as bad food in France. They wouldn't allow it."

Cecelia laughed and Deacon found himself trying to memorize the sound. He hadn't heard her laughter nearly enough when they were in Royal. He missed it. In their carefree younger days, she'd laughed freely and often. He wanted her to laugh more even if he wasn't around to hear it. That was part of the reason he'd brought her here—to get her away from the drama of home in the hopes he might catch a fleeting glimpse of the girl he'd once loved.

Not that he didn't appreciate the woman she'd become. The older, wiser, sexier Cecelia certainly had its benefits. Looking at her now, he could hardly keep his hands to himself. She was wearing a cream lace fitted sheath dress. It plunged deep, highlighting her ample cleavage, and clung to every womanly curve she'd developed while they were apart. Falling for Cecelia was the last thing on his mind when he arrived in Royal, but it was virtually impossible for him to keep his distance from her when she looked like that.

"Can we walk in the water?" she asked, surprising him.

"If you want to."

They both slipped out of their shoes, and Deacon rolled up his suit pants. He hadn't thought she would want to walk along the shore and let the sand ruin her new pedicure. Yet with her crystal embellished stilettos in her free hand, she tugged him off the stone path toward the water.

The cold water that washed over them was a shocking contrast to the warm sand on his bare feet. He expected Cecelia to bolt the moment the chill hit her, but instead, her eyes got big with excitement and she laughed again.

"It's a little chilly," he said.

"It's April. It feels good, though. I can't remember the last time I put my toes in the sand and walked through the surf. Too long."

Deacon felt momentarily sheepish. He couldn't

remember the last time he'd done it, either, and it was right outside his window the majority of the year.

"I understand why you'd rather be here than Royal," she said after they walked a good bit down the shoreline. "It's beautiful. And so different. I don't know that I want to go back, either." She chuckled and shook her head. "I will, but I don't want to."

Deacon felt the sudden urge to ask her why she couldn't stay. "Why go back?" he asked. "You don't have to do anything you don't want to do."

She looked at him through narrowed eyes. "Well, for one thing, I haven't finished your hotel yet. It opens in just a week and a half, if you'll recall. Plus, my company is in Royal. My employees. My friends and family."

"You could have all that here," he offered. "And me, too." Deacon surprised himself with the words, but he couldn't stop them from coming out. What would it be like to have her here with him all the time? Away from her parents' sphere of influence and the society nonsense she'd fallen prey to. He wanted to know.

Cecelia stopped walking, pulling him to a stop beside her. "You're not going to stay in Royal, are you?"

He shook his head. "You know I'm not."

Cecelia's gaze drifted into the distance. "I know. I guess a part of me was just hoping."

Deacon's heart sped in his chest. He hadn't given much thought to this fling with Cecelia lasting beyond the grand opening. He just couldn't disappoint himself that way. But it sounded like she was open to the possibility. "Hoping what?" he pressed.

"Hoping that you'd change your mind and stay awhile."

Deacon sighed. There were a lot of things he would do for her, but stay in Royal? He couldn't even imagine it. He didn't know why she'd ask him to, either. Didn't she realize how everyone treated him? How miserable it was for him? She didn't seem very happy there, either. "Royal, Texas, and I parted ways a long time ago."

Cecelia looked at him. "We parted ways, too, and yet here we are. Anything can happen."

He didn't want to argue about this and ruin their night. They were together now, and that was the most important thing. "You're right," he conceded. "Anything can happen. We'll see what the future brings."

Taking her hand into his, they started back down the beach. They were only a hundred yards or so from his hotel when he saw a child chasing after a dog on the beach. The little boy must've dropped the leash, and the large, wooly mutt seemed quite pleased with his newfound freedom.

In fact, the dog was heading right toward them. Before Deacon could react, the dog made a beeline for Cecelia. It jumped up, placing two dirty paw prints on her chest and knocking her off balance. Her hand slipped from his as she stumbled back and fell into the waves that were rushing up around their feet. She yelled as she tried—and failed—to find her footing in the icy water, soaking her dress and hair.

Deacon was in a panic and so was the little boy. They both lunged to pull the dog off her as it enthusiastically licked her face. It wasn't until the dog was yanked away that he realized Cecelia's shrieks were actually laughter. He stood, stunned for a moment by her reaction. Then he offered her his hand to lift her up out of the water, but she didn't take it. She was laughing too hard to care.

It was the damnedest thing he'd ever seen. The people back in Royal wouldn't believe it if Maverick circulated a picture of it. The perfect and poised Cecelia Morgan lying in the ocean fully clothed and covered in mud. The cream lace dress was absolutely ruined with dirty paw prints rubbed down the front. Her makeup was smeared across her skin, and her blond hair hung in damp tendrils around her face. She was a mess. But she didn't seem to care. And she couldn't have been more beautiful.

"*Je m'excuse, mademoiselle,*" the little boy said as he fought with the dog that weighed a good ten pounds more than he did. "*Mauvais chien!*" he chastised the pup, who finally sat down looking smug about the whole thing.

"Cecelia, are you okay?" Deacon asked. He wasn't sure what to do.

She struggled to catch her breath, then nodded. Her face was flushed bright red beneath the smears of her foundation and mascara. "I'm fine." She reached up for Deacon, and when he took her hand, she tugged hard, catching him off guard and jerking him down into the water with her.

"What the—" he complained as he pushed up from the water, soaked, but the joyful expression on her face stopped him. He rolled up to a seated position beside her. "Was that really necessary?" he asked.

She didn't answer him. Instead, she wrapped her arms around his neck and pulled him into a kiss. Deacon instantly forgot about the water, the dog, the cost of his ruined suit... All that mattered was the taste of Cecelia on his lips and the press of her body against his. She was uninhibited and free in his arms, kissing him with the same abandon she had that first night after her breakup with Chip.

There was no desperation this time, however. Just excitement and need.

He couldn't help but respond to it. This side of Cecelia was one he thought he might never see again. It was the side that had made out with him in the back of his truck, letting him get her hair and makeup all disheveled. It was the side that had sprayed him with the hose while he was detailing one of his restored cars and led to them getting covered in mud and grass as they wrestled on his front lawn.

Deacon had missed this Cecelia. Perfectly imperfect. Dirty. Joyful. Hot as hell. He realized that they weren't alone in the back of his truck, however. The little French boy and his dog were still standing there. He forced himself to pull away, looking over the mess she'd become.

The dress had been tight before, but wet, it was clingy and damn near see-through. He could see the hardened peaks of her nipples pressing through the fabric. He would have to give her his coat to cover her when they walked home.

"*Américains fous*," the little boy said with a dismayed shake of his head. He tugged on the dog's leash and headed back in the direction he'd come from.

"What did he say?" Cecelia asked.

"He called us crazy Americans." Deacon wiped

the water from his face and slicked back his hair. "I have to say I agree."

Cecelia giggled into her hand and looked down at her dress. Her fingers traced over some of the sand and mud embedded in the delicate lace and silk. "My mother just bought me this dress for Christmas. It was the first time I'd worn it. Oh, well."

"I'll buy you ten new dresses," he said. Deacon pushed himself up out of the water and helped her up, too. He slipped out of his suit coat, wringing out the water before placing it over her shoulders.

"I don't want more dresses," she said, pressing her body to his seductively with the little boy long gone. A wicked glint lit her eyes as her lips curled into a deceptively sweet smile. "I just want you. Right now."

Deacon swallowed hard. "I think this walk along the beach is over, don't you?"

Nine

"Where are we going?" Cecelia asked.

Deacon smiled from the driver's seat of his silver Renault Laguna. In France he drove a French car. It seemed appropriate. They were only about ten minutes outside the city, and she was already keen to know everything. "It's a surprise."

Cecelia pouted. "Isn't it enough of a surprise to bring me to France on a whim in the first place?"

Perhaps. But last night, he'd gotten a sneak peek at the Cecelia he'd fallen in love with. There, lying in the surf, covered in muddy paw prints and soaked to the bone with seawater, he'd seen a glimpse of her. The radiant smile, the flushed cheeks, the weight of the world lifted from her shoulders in that moment… He wanted to capture that feeling in a bottle for her so she could keep it forever and pull it out whenever she needed to.

It also helped him realize he was on the right track with her. Getting her away from Royal was the best thing he could've done. It wasn't enough, though. Now Deacon wanted to get her even farther from the city, farther from people, to see what she could be like if she could truly let loose. There was nothing like the fields of Provence for that.

It was the perfect day for a picnic. The skies were clear and a brilliant shade of blue. It was a warm spring day, with a light breeze that would keep them from getting overheated in the sun. It was the kind of day that beckoned him outside, and the chance to make love to Cecelia in a field of wildflowers under this same sky was an opportunity he couldn't pass up.

The hotel's kitchen had put together a picnic basket for them, and he'd hustled her into the car without a word. Cecelia hadn't seen him put the basket and blanket in the trunk, so she was stewing in her seat, wondering what they were up to. He liked torturing her just a little bit. She was always in charge of everything at her company. Today, he wanted her to just let him take care of her and enjoy herself for once.

Of course, if he'd told her they were going to Grasse, she wouldn't know what that was. It was a tiny, historic French town surrounded by lavender fields that fueled their local perfumeries. It was too early for the lavender to bloom—that wouldn't happen until late summer—but there would still be fields of grasses and wildflowers for them to sit in and enjoy with a lovely bottle of Provençal rosé.

He found a tiny gravel road that turned off into a field about a mile before they reached Grasse. He followed it, finding the perfect picnic spot beneath an old, weathered tree. He turned off the car and smiled at Cecelia's puzzled expression.

"Where are we?"

Deacon got out of the car and walked around to let her out. "Provence. It's the perfect afternoon for a picnic in the French countryside with a lovely lady such as yourself."

Cecelia smiled and took the hand he offered to climb out of the Renault. She was looking so beautiful today. Her long blond hair was loose in waves around her shoulders. It was never like that in Texas. She always kept it up in a bun or twist of some kind that was all business, no pleasure. He liked it down, where he could run his fingers through the golden silk of it.

She was also wearing a breezy sundress with a sweater that tugged just over her shoulders. The dress had a floral pattern of yellows and greens that pulled out the mossy tones in her eyes. It clung to her figure in a seductive but not overtly sexual way that made him want to slip the sweater off her shoulders and kiss the skin as he revealed it, inch by inch.

"It's beautiful here," she said as she tilted her face to the sun and let the breeze flutter her hair.

Deacon shut the door and opened the trunk. He handed her a blanket and pulled out the picnic basket. "Let's go over by the tree," he suggested.

They spread the blanket out and settled down onto it together. "In the summertime," he explained, "these fields will be overflowing with purple lavender. The scent is heavenly."

She looked around them, presumably trying to picture what it would look like in only a few months. "I can see why you choose to live here, Deacon. I mean, who wouldn't want to live in France if they had the chance? It's beautiful."

"The scenery is nice," he admitted, "but it can't hold a candle to your beauty. Texas seems to have the market on that, unfortunately."

Cecelia blushed and wrinkled her nose. She shook her head, dismissing his compliment. "You're sweet, but I don't believe a word of it. Not compared to something like this." She looked away from him to admire the landscape and avoid his gaze.

There were days when Deacon wished he could throttle her parents. She was one of the most perfect creatures he'd ever had the pleasure of meeting, and she didn't believe him because the Morgans were always pushing her to be better. That was impossible in his eyes. "You don't believe me? Why not? Am I prone to hollow compliments?"

"No, of course not. It's just because," she began, looking down at her hands instead of staring him in the eye, "this is one of the most beautiful places in the world. People dream their whole lives of visiting a place like this one day. I'm just a pretty girl."

"You're more than just a pretty girl, Cecelia." Deacon leaned in and dipped a finger beneath her chin to tilt her face up to his. He wanted to tell her how smart and talented and amazing she was, but he could tell by the hard glint in her eye that she wouldn't believe him. Could she not tell by the way he responded to her touch? How he looked at her like she was the most delectable pastry in the window of Ladurée?

"What do we have to eat?" she asked, pulling away from his touch and focusing on the picnic basket.

"I'm not entirely sure," he admitted, letting the

conversation drop for now. "The head chef put this together for me, so it's a surprise for us both."

Deacon opened the lid and reached inside, pulling out one container after the next. There was niçoise salad with hard-boiled eggs, olives, tuna, potatoes and green beans. Another contained carrot slaw with Dijon mustard and chives. Brown parchment paper was wrapped around a bundle of savory puff pastries stuffed with multicolored grape tomatoes, goat cheese and drizzled with a reduction of balsamic vinegar and honey. Another bundle of crostini was paired with a ramekin of chicken pâté.

Finally, he pulled out a little box with a variety of French macarons for dessert. It was quite the feast, and very much the kind of picnic she'd likely never experienced back in Texas. There was more to food than barbecue, although you could never convince a Texan of that.

They spent the next hour enjoying their lunch. Together, they devoured almost every crumb. They laughed and talked as they ate, feeding each other bites and reminding him of that afternoon they shared at the Silver Saddle. Their second chance had truly started that afternoon with a tableful of tapas between them.

Now, a week later, here they were. This was not at all what Deacon had expected when he agreed to build The Bellamy with Shane and return to Royal.

Sure, he knew he would see Cecelia. He figured they would converse politely and briefly over the course of their work together at the hotel, but never did he think he would touch her. Kiss her. Lose himself inside her.

He hadn't let himself fantasize about something like that because it hadn't seemed possible when he left Royal behind all those years ago. Then she'd shown up on his doorstep, devastated and suddenly single, and everything changed. Was it possible that he'd succeeded in being good enough for a woman like her? A part of him still couldn't believe it.

"What is it?" Cecelia asked. "You're staring at me. Do I have something on my face?"

Deacon shook his head. "Not at all. I was just thinking about how lucky I am to be here today with a woman as amazing as you are."

He expected the same reaction as before, but this time, when she looked into his eyes, the hard resistance there was gone. Did she finally believe him? He hoped so.

Cecelia thanked him by leaning close and pressing her lips to his. He drank her in, enjoying the taste of her, even as he slipped the sweater from her shoulders as he'd fantasized doing earlier. He tore his mouth from hers so he could kiss a path on the line of her jaw, down her throat and across the bare shoulder he'd exposed. She sighed and leaned into his touch.

"I was such a stupid little girl back then," she said with a wistful sigh. "All this time I could've had you, and I ruined everything. I don't know if I can ever forgive myself for that. Can you?"

Deacon's gaze met hers. "Yes," he said without wavering. It was true. As long as they ended up right here, right now, who cared about the past anymore?

Reaching out, Deacon swiped all the containers and food wrappers out of his way, leaving a bare expanse of blanket to lay Cecelia down on. Her blond hair fanned across the pale blue wool as she laid back and looked up at him with her mossy, gray-green eyes and soft smile.

"What are you doing?" she asked as he hooked a finger beneath the strap of her dress and pulled it down her arm.

Her right breast was on the verge of being exposed, and his mouth watered at the sight of her pink nipple just peeking out from the edge of her dress. He didn't answer her. Instead, he leaned down and tugged the fabric until he could draw that same nipple into his mouth. Cecelia gasped and arched her back, pressing her flesh closer to him.

"Someone could see us out here," Cecelia said half-heartedly. She certainly wasn't pushing him away.

"Do you want me to stop?" he asked, ceasing the pleasurable nibbling of her flesh.

"No," she whispered, excitement brightening her eyes.

"Good. Let them see us. I'm about to make love to you, Cecelia, and I don't care who knows about it."

It had been a long time since Cecelia had made love in a public place, and even then, it had been in the back of Deacon's old pickup truck while they parked in a secluded area by the lake on a Friday night. This wasn't quite as private, and it was broad daylight, but there was no way she would tell him no. Not when he looked at her the way he did and said things that made her resistance as weak as her knees.

If she were being honest with herself, she couldn't say no to Deacon, no matter what he asked of her. He was her knight in shining armor; the prince who swooped in and saved her when she felt like the walls of her life were tumbling down around her. She would give him anything he asked of her, even her heart.

She looked up at Deacon as he smiled mischievously at her and returned to feasting on her sensitive breasts. He still looked so much like the boy she remembered, even if he had grown into such a handsome and successful man. It made her think of the days and nights she'd spent in his arms and the future they'd planned together all those years ago. They'd both accomplished more than they'd ever dared to dream, but they'd both done it alone.

Cecelia didn't want to do it alone anymore. She wanted to live her life and chase her dreams with Deacon by her side. She felt her chest tighten as she realized that Deacon didn't need to ask for her heart. He already had it, even if he didn't know it. She was head over heels in love with him, even after such a short time together. It made her wonder if she had ever truly stopped loving him.

Her parents had been behind the breakup. She had done what she had to do, putting her feelings for Deacon on a shelf to protect her heart, but they'd never truly gone away. She hadn't loved anyone else. How could she? Cecelia had given her heart to him back in high school.

Deacon looked down at her, bringing her focus back to the here and now. She ran her fingers through the dark blond waves of his hair and then tugged him to her. He didn't resist, dipping his head to kiss her. Cecelia felt the last of her resolve dissipate. She wasn't strong enough to keep fighting her feelings and denying what they had. She was out of reasons not to love him. Out of reasons to push him away. She had to travel to the other side of the earth to feel like she was in control of her own life, but she wasn't going back to the way she was before they left Royal.

She was in love with Deacon, and she didn't care who knew it. It was really none of their damn business. Just as her birth mother's identity, and the challenges she'd had to face, was none of their business. Considering all the dirt Maverick was digging up on people in Royal, the residents of her small town really needed to tend to their own gardens and stop worrying about hers.

They broke the kiss, and a sly grin curled his lips. She could feel his hand gliding up her bare leg, pushing the hem of her long cotton dress higher and higher.

"Yes," she encouraged when his fingertips brushed along the edge of her lace panties. "I don't want to wait any longer."

Not to have him inside her. Not to have him in her life. Not to love him with all her heart and soul. She'd spent her whole life waiting for this.

Deacon removed her panties and flung them unceremoniously into the picnic basket. With his green-gold eyes solely focused on her, he traveled down her body, pressing kisses against her exposed breasts, her cotton-clad stomach and down where her panties had once been.

He parted her thighs and continued to look right at her as he leaned down to take a quick taste of her.

Cecelia gasped as the bolt of pleasure shot straight through her. She was both thrilled and horrified by the idea of doing something like this outdoors in broad daylight. She wasn't a prude, but there was something so intimate about the contact that it seemed like the kind of thing that should be done in the semidarkness of her bedroom.

Deacon didn't seem to care where they were. His tongue flicked across her flesh again before he began stroking her sensitive center with abandon. There was nothing Cecelia could do to stop the roller coaster she found herself on. She gripped the blanket tightly in her fists, hoping it was strong enough to hold her to the earth.

Deacon was relentless. His fingers and his tongue stroked, probed, teased and tortured her until her breath was passing through her lips in strangled sobs. Her whole body was tense from the buildup inside her. She tried to hold back, to prolong the feeling as long as she could, but she couldn't. He stroked hard and slipped a finger inside her at the perfect moment, and she came undone. Deacon held her hips, tightly gripping them to continue his pleasurable assault even as she writhed and trembled beneath him.

"Please," she gasped at last when she couldn't take any more. "I can't."

Only then did he pull away, allowing her to finally relax into the blanket. She closed her eyes and reveled in the way her body felt fluid, almost boneless, as she lay there. Her climax had seemingly stripped her of the capacity to move. The sun was warm on her bare skin, heating the outside of her even as her insides were near the boiling point.

She was barely cognizant of Deacon hovering near her, and she pried open her eyes. He was propped on his elbow, looking down at her with mild concern.

"Are you okay?" he asked.

"I'll be better when you're inside me," she replied, her voice a hoarse whisper after her earlier shouts.

"I thought you might need a minute." Deacon grinned.

"All I need is you," Cecelia said, and she'd never meant words more in her life. He was all she wanted. In her bed, in her life, in her heart.

"If you say so."

Cecelia shifted her hips and pulled her dress out of the way so he could position himself between her thighs. He fumbled with his pants for a moment, and then she got what she wanted. He filled her hard and fast, freezing in place once he was as deep as he could go.

She watched as he closed his eyes and gritted his teeth, savoring the feeling of being inside her.

"Do you know," Deacon began without moving an inch, "you feel exactly the same way you did when you were seventeen? It takes damn near everything I have not to spill into you right now, you're so tight."

Instead of responding, she drew her knees up to cradle his hips and tightened her muscles around him.

"Damn," he groaned and made an almost pained expression as he fought to keep control.

She didn't care. He'd certainly shown no mercy when she was resisting her release, and she wasn't about to, either. She lifted her hips, allowing him in a fraction of an inch farther.

He blew air hard through his nose and shook his head in defiance. "Not yet, Cecelia. Not yet. When I go, you're coming with me." Deacon bent down and pressed his lips against hers. She wrapped her arms around his neck and held him tight enough that her breasts flattened against the starched cotton of his green button-down shirt.

His tongue slipped over her bottom lip and into her mouth. Slowly, he stroked her tongue with his own. Cecelia expected him to mirror the rhythm with his hips, but he was frustratingly still from the waist down.

Unable to take any more of his slow torture, she pulled away from his kiss, leaving only the tiniest fraction of an inch between his lips and hers. "If you want me, Deacon, take me. I'm yours. I always have been."

That was as close to "I love you" as she was willing to go. At least for now. It was early to confess her feelings, and if he took the news poorly, she'd be stranded in a foreign country. No, that was a revelation best left to her hometown. He'd be more likely to believe her there as opposed to it being some kind of vacation-fling confession. Hell, she'd be more likely to believe herself there, too.

Her words had the intended reaction. Deacon buried his face in the small of her neck, planted a kiss just below her ear, then began to move inside her. It was slow and sweet at first, but before long, he was thrusting hard. The small break they'd taken allowed him to continue on, but she could tell by the tense muscles of his neck and the pinched expression on his face that it wouldn't be long.

She wouldn't be long, either. Despite just recovering from her orgasm only minutes earlier, she could feel another release building. She clutched Deacon's broad back and lifted her hips for the greatest impact. That was enough to make both of them groan with renewed pleasure.

"Yes, please, Deacon," she whispered into the summer breeze.

He didn't need the encouragement to act. Deacon reached between them and stroked her center as he continued to thrust into her. His fingers quickly brought her to the edge, making her scream.

Cecelia quickly buried her face in his shoulder to smother the cries before they drew someone's attention. Yet there was no way to smother the sensations running through her body. An intense wave of pleasure pulsated through every inch of her, curling her toes and making her fingertips tingle. Her heart tightened in her chest, reminding her just how different it was to make love instead of just having sex. It had been so long that she forgot there was a difference.

Her flutter of release sent Deacon over the edge. With a roar, he spilled himself into her and collapsed, pressing her into the blanket.

Cecelia held him against her bare bosom as their breathing returned to normal and their heart rates slowed together. As she held him, she looked up at the brilliant blue sky and wished this moment could last forever.

Unfortunately, the time together in France was coming to an end. It was time to fly back to Royal, debut The Bellamy and face the music.

Ten

Everything was perfect.

The hotel was flawless for its big debut. The black-tie-attired crowd filled the lobby of The Bellamy, flowing into the ballroom and out to the courtyard surrounding the pool. Even then it was almost elbow to elbow. It seemed as though the whole town had shown up to get their first peek at the resort. Unfazed by the crowd, the waiters moved expertly through guests with trays of delicious tapas and signature cocktails.

Shane and Brandee were beaming, and rightfully so. Deacon had heard nothing but compliments on the hotel so far. People loved the design, loved the food and couldn't wait to have guests stay at The Bellamy. Even people who at one time might've given Deacon dirty looks as they passed on the sidewalk stopped to congratulate him.

It was exactly what Royal needed, he was told. He certainly hoped so. He and Shane had a lot of money tied up in this place, and he hoped to get it back. If he could finally coexist with the upper-class circles of Royal, that would be even better. Maybe he'd be willing to stay a little longer than he'd planned after all. Deacon wasn't ready to make any big decisions, but the more time he spent in Royal, the easier it became. Cecelia might just talk him into becoming a Texan again before too long.

The only wrong tonight was the fact that he couldn't find Cecelia anywhere. Things had been crazy the minute they'd touched down in Texas. Their relaxing, romantic vacation came to a quick end with the final week of preparations that needed to be made for the opening of the resort.

He'd gotten used to having her in his bed and by his side, so it pained him to have her suddenly ripped away. He didn't even know what she was wearing tonight or if she was even here yet. He thought he saw her blonde head in the crowd, but he hadn't managed to get his hands on her with everyone wanting to congratulate him on the hotel.

"Mr. Chase?"

Deacon turned and found Brent and Tilly Morgan, of all people, waiting to speak to him. He made a poor attempt to mask his surprise, smiling and shaking Brent's hand although he had no idea why they wanted to talk to him. They never wanted anything to do with him before, and they certainly had never wanted him anywhere near their daughter.

"Mr. and Mrs. Morgan, so glad you could make it. How do you like the hotel?"

"It really is lovely," Tilly said. "Cecelia refused to give us any hints about her design, but I can see her refined aesthetic here in the lobby. I would love to see one of the guest rooms. Are any of them open to view?"

Deacon nodded, ignoring the fact that all of Tilly's compliments about the hotel were focused on their daughter's work and not on anything that had to do with him. "There's a gentleman near the elevators who is escorting guests to one of her suites on the second floor if you would like to take a tour. Cecelia really did an amazing job. Shane and I had no doubts in her ability to execute our vision here for The Bellamy. You should be very proud of her."

"Oh, we are," a man said from over Tilly's shoulder.

It'd been quite a few years since Deacon had laid eyes on Chip Ashford, but he instantly recognized him. Tall, blond...the perfect golden boy with an arrogant smirk and a spray-on tan. The people in Royal saw him as some sort of god, but he just looked like a game show host to Deacon—all smiles and no authenticity.

Deacon wasn't about to let Chip's treatment of Cecelia go unnoted after he stood there gloating about her as though they were still engaged. "I'm surprised to hear you say that, Chip. From what Cecelia tells me, you two didn't part very well. Something about her being an imposter."

"That was just a little misunderstanding," Chip said dismissively. "Wasn't it, Brent?"

Cecelia's father immediately nodded, as though he'd almost been coached with his response. "A little bit of nothing. Cecelia tends to get upset about the silliest things and make them into a bigger deal than they are. Nothing more than a little lover's spat."

Tilly nodded enthusiastically. Deacon was disgusted by how they sucked up to the Ashfords. The Morgans were a fine family on their own, and frankly, it was embarrassing.

"Brent, why don't you take Tilly upstairs to see one of Cecelia's rooms? I'd like to have a private chat with Deacon, if you don't mind."

"Not at all, not at all. Come on, Tilly." Brent put his arm around his wife and escorted her through the crowd to the wall of brass elevator doors that led upstairs.

Deacon watched them disappear, curious about what Chip had to say to him in private. The two of them had probably shared less than a dozen words between them. He imagined there was only one thing that Chip wanted to talk about: Cecelia. She was the only thing they had ever had in common.

The friendly expression on Chip's face vanished the moment the Morgans disappeared. When he turned back to look at Deacon, a scowl lined his forehead and drew down the corners of his mouth. "I've heard that you've been taking up with Cecelia."

Deacon did his best to maintain a neutral expression. He didn't want to give Chip any ammunition. "Have you? Good news travels fast."

"I wouldn't consider you making moves on my fiancée to be good news. Because of that whole dustup about the adoption, I am willing to be a gentleman and overlook the whole thing between you two. Especially since Cecelia has come to her senses."

Deacon tensed up and frowned at Chip's statement. "Come to her senses and realized marrying you was an epic mistake?"

Chip snorted in derision. "Hardly. You see, Chase, while you were busy getting ready to open this hotel, I was busy reconciling with my fiancée. I'll admit I reacted poorly to her news, but I apologized to her and she's accepted my apology. I presume, now that the hotel is open and the engagement is back on, that you'll crawl back into whatever European hole you climbed out of."

Deacon could hardly believe his ears. Chip couldn't be serious. There was no way that Cecelia would take him back after the way he had treated her. Deacon had been the one who'd comforted her when Chip broke their engagement. Deacon had been the one who'd whisked her away to France to avoid the cutting gossip after Maverick's revelation about her adoption. Deacon was the one who had held her in his arms, worshipped her body and accepted her for who she really was.

Would she really go back to the man who had shunned her after nothing more than a simple apology?

"You look surprised, Chase. I take it Cecelia hasn't gotten a chance to break the bad news to you yet. I would imagine the truth smarts a little, but you can't really be surprised. We all know who gets the girl in this scenario. I don't care how much money you've made over the years or who you've conned to get it. She wants a man from a good family with the connections and the power that only someone like I can give her. You might be a fun diversion in the sack, but you'll never be enough of a man in her eyes for anything more serious than that."

Deacon tried not to flinch at Chip's expertly aimed barb. Without fail, it hit him right in his most tender spot. He had worked hard to make more of himself, to be the man Cecelia always thought he could be. But he had always wondered if that was enough. It hadn't been enough back in high school when she broke up with him. She hadn't given him any reason to doubt her, but what really made him think that anything had changed?

Chip was right. He had money. But there were some things that money couldn't buy, things that Chip had been born with. If that really was the most important thing to her, Deacon would never be good enough.

"Besides, I've been doing a lot of thinking and talking to my campaign manager, and we've decided that her past isn't the career bombshell I thought it might be. In fact, it might even be an advantage. I'm not polling well with the working-class demographic. Having a fiancée with a tragic backstory like hers—adopted with a drug-addicted mother and humble origins—might give me an edge come election time. It makes me more relatable to the masses."

Deacon looked at Chip's smug expression and

felt his hands curl into fists at his side. Cecelia was nothing more than a campaign prop to him. Chip might be more connected than him, but he wasn't stronger. He had no doubt that he could lay Chip out on the floor without much effort. It would be amazingly gratifying to feel his knuckles pound into the man's jaw. He could just imagine the stunned looks on the faces of everyone around them as Chip lay bleeding on the newly laid marble floor.

But he wouldn't do that. He liked to think that he'd gained some class along with his money over the years. Starting a brawl at the opening gala of his five-star resort wouldn't earn him any new friends in this town. He wouldn't ruin this night for Shane and Brandee, or any of the hotel's employees. They had all worked too hard to make tonight a success, and he didn't want to undo their efforts with his brash behavior. Chip wasn't worth it.

Besides, if Chip *was* telling the truth and Cecelia had chosen to return to him after everything he'd done to her…she wasn't the woman he loved. The Cecelia he wanted was the one he'd fallen for again in Cannes. There, she had been happy and free of all the pressures this damned town put on her. That woman wouldn't have returned to Chip after his cold betrayal. But perhaps that woman had stayed behind in France.

Deacon eyed Chip coolly before swallowing his

pride and holding out his hand like a gentleman would. "Well, congratulations on your engagement. You two certainly deserve each other."

Chip narrowed his gaze at Deacon's backhanded compliment, but chose to grin and accept it anyway.

"If you'll excuse me," Deacon said, walking away before Chip could respond. He had to get away from him before he reconsidered punching him in the face. Instead, he sought out Shane and Brandee. He knew this was his party, too, but he couldn't stand to be here another moment. He certainly didn't want to be a witness to Cecelia and Chip's reconciliation. Seeing her on that bastard's arm was more than he could take. It was better that he leave now than risk causing a scene and ruining the whole night.

When he found Shane, he leaned in and whispered a few things to him. Shane turned to him with a surprised look on his face but knew better than to start a discussion about it right now. He simply nodded and clapped Deacon on the shoulder.

Deacon turned and disappeared into the bowels of the hotel where only staff were allowed to go. He wasn't entirely sure where he was headed, he just knew that he had to put some distance between himself and the woman he had been foolish enough to fall in love with the second time.

Shame on him.

* * *

Cecelia circled the ballroom for the third time, still unsuccessful in locating Deacon. She had been anxious about tonight—her first public appearance since Maverick spilled her secrets—but as she maneuvered through the crowd, everyone had carried on as if nothing had happened.

She was glad because she refused to have tonight ruined by old drama that was out of her control. She had more important things to tend to. She was bubbling over with nerves and excitement, eager to find Deacon, but so far she was having no luck. She was certain he was here—she had seen him earlier, and his car was still in the lot—but now he had vanished into thin air.

Arriving late to the party had not been a part of her plan for the evening, but it had been unavoidable. She'd had to make an unplanned stop to confirm something she had suspected since they got back from Cannes. Now that she knew for certain, she couldn't wait to find Deacon, but he was lost in a sea of tuxedos and cocktail dresses.

She was on the way to the office suites to see if he was hiding out and working instead of enjoying the party. That was when she found herself face-to-face with her ex-fiancé in a secluded hallway.

Chip was wearing his favorite Armani tuxedo, showing off his good looks the way he'd always liked to do. There had been a time when Cecelia could have been swayed by his handsome appearance, but that was in the past. There was no comparison between him and Deacon, and she couldn't understand how she let herself waste so much time on a man with few redeeming qualities outside of his social standing.

"There you are, kitten. I have been looking all over for you, tonight."

Cecelia folded her arms over her chest and narrowed her gaze at him. "I can't imagine why. And please don't use pet names, Chip. I'm not your kitten. I'm not your anything, if you recall us breaking up a few weeks ago."

Chip smiled, oozing all the practiced charm that he used on women and constituents alike. "Listen, I'm sorry about how all that went down. It was wrong of me, and I reacted poorly."

Cecelia was stunned by his apology, although it meant very little to her now. She didn't understand why he was bothering her, much less cornering her at the opening, when she had more important things to be doing. What was he after? "Thank you. Now if you'll excuse me I—"

Chip reached out and caught her arm, stopping her from pushing past him and returning to the party. "What's the rush, kitten? We really need to talk about some things. I've been doing a lot of thinking about us."

"Us? We don't have anything to talk about, Chip, but especially not about *us*." Cecelia was desperate to escape, jerking away from his grasp. She glanced over his shoulder, hoping to catch the eye of anybody who could come and rescue her, but there was no one in sight. The party was carrying on at the other end of the hallway. "I would rather have a root canal than talk to you right now."

Chip just smiled. "My favorite part of my kitten is her claws. Now just relax and give me five minutes. We were together a long time, certainly you can spare a moment or two. That's all I ask."

Cecelia sighed. "Okay, fine. Five minutes, that's it. And stop calling me kitten. Do it one more time and I walk."

He held up his hands defensively. "Okay, okay. No more pet names. Cecelia, I came here looking for you tonight because the last few weeks apart have helped me realize that I was a fool. My feelings for you are stronger than I thought, even stronger than my concerns about your background. I've realized they're unfounded. I need you by my side going into this next reelection."

Cecelia could hardly believe her ears. When she was a liability, he couldn't dump her fast enough. Now that he decided she could be an asset to his campaign, he was crawling back. He was delusional to think she would go along with nonsense like this. "Chip, you've lost your mind."

"No, hear me out. You and I are good together. We always have been. We make the perfect American couple. Voters are just going to eat up the classic, traditional values we represent. This is a win-win for us both, Cecelia."

She could only shake her head. "You never wanted *me*, Chip. You just wanted some trophy wife you can parade around at fund-raisers and rallies. That's not what I want out of my marriage."

Chip didn't look dissuaded. He was well versed in debate, and she could tell that he wasn't going to give up until he won. "It wasn't so long ago that I was everything you wanted, Cecelia. You were so anxious to plan our wedding and start our life together. What about the children we were going to have? The future we planned? Are you willing to just throw all that away?"

"You threw it away, Chip, not me. And yes, I am willing to walk away from what you've offered me. I have found something infinitely better."

Chip chuckled bitterly. "You mean Deacon? Seriously? I'm offering you the chance to be the first lady of the United States, Cecelia. I'm going all the way to the White House one day, and I want to take you with me." He reached into his pocket and pulled out the engagement ring she'd returned the afternoon they broke up. He held it up like a gaudy offering to the diamond gods. "You're going to turn this down and walk away from the amazing life that we have ahead of us because you've got feelings for that loser?"

"As a matter of fact I am, Chip. Your five minutes are up." Cecelia brushed past him and the engagement ring she'd once worn and pushed into the crowd, hoping he didn't follow her. How she ever could've agreed to marry a man like that was beyond her. What was she thinking? She knew. It was what her parents wanted for her. She was tired of that. Now she wanted what she wanted for herself, whether they liked it or not.

She was about to start a new phase in her life, and she wanted to start it with Deacon. *If* she could find him. Finally, she spotted Shane and went up to him, hoping he could help her track Deacon down.

Shane spotted her and smiled in a polite, yet oddly cold fashion. "Good evening, Cecelia."

"Evening, Shane. Have you seen Deacon anywhere? I've been looking for him all night, and I haven't managed to find him."

Shane nodded. "Deacon had to leave, but he told me to tell you congratulations on your engagement."

Cecelia's blood went ice-cold in her veins. "What engagement?" she asked.

"You and Chip. Both he and your parents have been telling everybody at the party that you two have reconciled and the wedding is back on. It's all anyone can talk about tonight. Quite a shrewd tactic to suppress the other scandal, I have to say."

Her jaw dropped. She couldn't even believe what she was hearing. Chip was such an arrogant bastard that he'd gone around announcing their engagement before he'd even talked to her about it. How dare he tell people that they got back together without even consulting her! "I can't believe this," she said. And then she realized the depth of what this meant.

Deacon thought that she had taken Chip back. How could he believe such a thing? He hadn't even asked her if it were true. No wonder he had left the party early. She dropped her head into her hands and groaned.

"What's the matter?" Shane asked.

She couldn't even answer him. She didn't want to waste another minute talking to him when she could be tracking down Deacon and clearing up this whole mess. She turned and ran as fast as she could, weaving through the crowd to find the nearest exit and get to her car.

Cecelia was almost out of the ballroom when she heard her father's sharp, demanding voice say her name. She stopped and turned, seeing her parents standing a few feet away with a typically disappointed expression on their faces. "I can't talk right now, Dad."

"You can and you will, young lady. Chip tells us that you turned your nose up at his apology and proposal. What are you thinking? Do you know how hard we had to work to stay in the Ashfords' good graces after all this blew up? After Maverick released your information, you were nowhere to be found. Your mother and I had to deal with the backlash."

"Please reconsider, dear," her mother said in a less authoritative tone. "I really do think Chip is a good choice for you. He has so much potential, and he's from such a good family. We should be thankful that they're willing to reconsider the engagement after the truth about your lineage came to light. What are they going to think when Chip tells them that you've rejected him for the son of a mechanic?"

Cecelia's hands curled into fists at her side. If she'd gotten nothing else from her time in Cannes, it was that she wasn't going to let her life be dictated by her parents anymore. "Honestly, I really don't care what they think of me. I don't want anything to do with them, much less become one of them. I am not marrying Chip Ashford. If he hasn't ruined it for me tonight, I intend to marry Deacon Chase."

Both her parents looked at her with an expression

of shock and dismay, but she didn't care. She cut her father off before he could start telling her why she was wrong. "I am tired of working so hard to meet your approval. If you truly love me, you will love and accept me for who I am, not for who you want me to be, and certainly not for whom I do or do not marry. If you can't agree to that, then I don't want you in my life any longer."

She didn't wait for their response. Right now, all that mattered was finding Deacon. Outside the ballroom, Cecelia slipped out of her high heels and ran through the back door of the hotel with them clutched in her hand.

She scanned the parking lot, but she didn't see his Corvette anywhere now. She rushed over to her own car and headed straight for his place. When she pulled up the gravel driveway, she was disappointed to find his car wasn't there, either, and all the lights were out. He'd told Shane he was leaving. Cecelia thought he had meant he was leaving the party, but now she had a sick ache in her stomach that made her think that perhaps he meant he was leaving Royal altogether.

She whipped her car back out onto the highway and rushed to the small executive airport where he had chartered the private jet to take them to France. If he was really, truly leaving, his car would be there.

At the airport, she found only more disappointment. The airport was mostly empty, with only one other car in the parking lot, and it wasn't Deacon's. She put her car in Park and sat there, unsure of what to do next. She didn't know where else to look for him.

Frustrated, she leaned back into her seat and let her tears flow freely down her cheeks. This was not the way she envisioned tonight going. Tonight was supposed to be happy. She was supposed to be sharing the most amazing and exciting news with the man she loved, and instead she was sitting in an empty parking lot alone, feeling as though everything she had ever wanted in life was slipping through her fingers.

Her whole life, all she ever wanted was her own family. Blood, love and a bond that nothing could split apart. Today, when she'd gotten home from the drugstore, she had looked at the two lines on the pregnancy test and thought that her dream was finally coming true. She had rushed to The Bellamy, anxious to share the good news with Deacon, only to have her dream intercepted by her delusional, lying ex.

And now, if she didn't find a way to clear things up with Deacon, she was going to find herself in a position she never expected: a single mother.

Eleven

Deacon was nowhere to be found.

It'd been three days since the grand opening of The Bellamy, and no one, not even Shane, had seen him. Or at least that's what he'd said. He wasn't likely to roll on his friend if his friend didn't want to be found. Deacon hadn't shown up at the hotel offices to work. His laptop was missing from his docking station. He hadn't been seen at his house. It was like he had simply vanished off the face of the earth.

Cecelia had tried contacting him on his cell phone, but he wasn't responding to her calls or texts. She didn't even think his phone was turned on because it immediately rolled to voice mail. That or he'd blocked her. She supposed that if she dropped the news on him in a text, he would respond. However, it just seemed wrong to tell a man he's going to be a father that way.

She caught herself constantly checking her phone for a missed message, each time frowning in disappointment and putting the phone back down. When her phone did ring, it was people she didn't want to talk to. Her father was too stubborn to reach out, but her mother had called three times and left messages. Still, Cecelia wasn't quite ready to speak to them. They had sold her out to get back in the Ashfords' good graces, and it would be a long time before Cecelia would be calm enough to sit down with them and have an adult conversation about how she planned to live her life from now on. If they ever wanted to see their grandchild, they'd adjust to the new Cecelia pretty quickly.

She was even ignoring calls from Naomi and Simone. She knew if she spoke to them she would spill the news about the baby, and Deacon needed to be the first to know, no question.

She was starting to get desperate. With the job at The Bellamy complete, Cecelia had moved back into her business offices. Now was the time that she was supposed to leverage her high-profile job at The Bellamy and launch her adult furniture line, but she found her heart just wasn't in it. It required a level of dedication and focus that she simply didn't have at the moment. Perhaps it was pregnancy brain. She'd heard that it could cause difficulty concentrating.

Or maybe it was simply the fact that Chip had potentially ruined the future she'd always wanted with Deacon. That made everything, including the success of Luna Fine Furnishings, seem insignificant in comparison.

Sitting back in her office chair, Cecelia gently stroked her flat belly. Her doctor, Janine Fetter, had calculated her to be four weeks along, but she would be showing before she knew it. How was it that her life had changed so drastically in such a short period of time? It seemed like only yesterday that she was getting ready to pitch her designs for The Bellamy to Shane, planning her wedding with Chip and paying off Maverick with blackmail money.

Now the job at the hotel was over, her engagement was broken, her secrets were public knowledge and she was pregnant with the child of a man who seemingly didn't want her any longer. She supposed she could blame the entire situation on Maverick. If he hadn't started meddling in her life, she wouldn't have had to confess to Chip and break their engagement. She wouldn't have thrown herself at Deacon because he was the only one who knew the truth and wouldn't judge her. She wouldn't have hopped on a flight to France with him to avoid the backlash of her secret being exposed to the entire town. She wouldn't have fallen in love with him again in a lavender field.

She also wouldn't be pregnant. It was a little ironic that the one thing she'd always wanted, the baby she'd dreamed of since she was a teenager, had come to be through the complicated machinations of the town blackmailer. If she ever found out who was behind it all, she supposed she should send him an invitation to the baby shower.

Cecelia's stomach started to sour. She reached for the roll of antacids in her desk drawer only to find she'd chewed the last one an hour ago. She didn't know whether it was thinking about Maverick or the latest in her constant bouts of morning sickness, but the Rolaids and saltine crackers she'd been eating lately weren't cutting it. At this rate, she'd be the first pregnant woman in history to lose weight.

With a sigh, she slammed the drawer shut and eyed the clock on her computer monitor. It was almost lunchtime. Time to run a few errands. She needed to go in search of something nausea friendly like chicken noodle soup and maybe a big glass of ginger ale to go with it. Her next stop would be the drugstore to restock her medicinal supplies before heading back to the office.

Pushing away from her desk, Cecelia picked up her purse and swung it over her shoulder. The offices of To the Moon were fairly close to downtown Royal, so she was able to walk the two blocks to the Royal Diner.

The Royal Diner was one of the few places in the town proper to eat, or at least it had been before The Bellamy opened with their high-class offerings. The diner was far more informal, complete with a retro '50s style. As Cecelia stepped in, the sheriff's wife and owner, Amanda Battle, waved at her from behind the counter. She opted for one of the unoccupied red leather booths. Sitting at the counter would invite too much conversation, and her heart just wasn't in it today.

There was chicken and wild rice soup on the menu. She ordered a bowl of that with crackers and a ginger ale. Amanda wrote down the order and eyed her critically, but didn't ask whatever questions were on the tip of her tongue.

Amanda returned with a tray a few minutes later and started unloading everything. "I brought extra crackers," she said, her tone pointed. "You look like you need them."

Cecelia looked up at her, wondering if she looked that awful. "Thank you."

"When I was pregnant," Amanda began, "I had the worst morning sickness you can imagine. Do you know what helped?"

Cecelia tried not to stiffen in her seat. Why was Amanda telling her this? It was one thing for her to look green around the gills, another for the woman to know she was pregnant.

"Those bracelets they give you when you go on a cruise. It puts pressure on some part of your wrist that makes the nausea go away. You can get them at the drugstore. If it wasn't for those and ginger ale, I might've never made it to the second trimester. That one is a lot more fun."

"Thank you," Cecelia repeated. "I'll look into that."

Amanda smiled, seemingly content to help and not at all concerned about the juiciness of the information she had inadvertently unearthed. "I'm glad you've got some new joy coming into your life. I felt so bad over those posts about your birth mother. That stupid Maverick can't ruin everything, no matter how hard he might try."

At that, Amanda turned and walked away, leaving Cecelia with her soup and her thoughts. She was right. Everything was a mess at the moment, but she knew things would work out.

Perking up in her seat, Cecelia had a thought. Maverick had managed to spread gossip to damn near everyone in town with hardly any effort at all. Maybe she could use his tricks to get Deacon back, as well. The power of social media had worked well for him, so why wouldn't it work for her?

Cecelia quickly finished her lunch, left money for the tab on the table and headed down the street to the drugstore. The morning sickness that had dominated her thoughts faded to the back of her mind as she formulated her plan with each step. She quickly restocked her supply of antacids, grabbed a bottle of prenatal vitamins and, on Amanda's recommendation, picked up a special nausea wristband designed for pregnant women.

After checking out, she rushed back to the office and immediately started drafting a message. She kept it short and sweet, using Maverick's hashtag. Plenty of people in town were following it, so the news should spread like wildfire. And, if Maverick himself was a little perturbed that he hadn't managed to ruin her life by exposing her latest tidbit of gossip, all the better.

She started with Snapchat and a photo of her bare ring finger. She followed it up with Instagram and Twitter. Finally, she posted to Facebook. Everyone in town, including her parents, the Ashfords

and Deacon himself, should be using one or more
of those platforms.

*"Despite persistent rumors to the contrary, I
am not, and never will be, engaged to Chip Ashford ever again. I would much rather be Mrs. Deacon Chase, and I hope that after everything that
has happened between us, he will believe that and
know how much I love him."*

That done, she sat back in her chair and hoped
for the best. There was a new flutter of butterflies
in her stomach, but this time it had nothing to do
with morning sickness and everything to do with
putting her heart on the line. Every word of the
post was true. Even if Deacon never looked in her
direction after what happened, she wasn't about to
go back to the life she'd escaped with the Ashfords.
Being with Deacon had helped her to realize that
there was more to a relationship than arm candy
and photo ops.

She wanted a real, loving relationship with a man
who respected and appreciated her no matter what.
And she knew now, more than ever, that she wanted
that relationship with Deacon. Their baby would be
the icing on the cake, completing the family she'd
always wanted.

Surely Deacon didn't really believe that she
would take Chip back after everything he had done
to her? He'd torn off, taking Chip at his word. She

couldn't imagine what Chip had said to him to send him into hiding without even asking her first. If she knew, Chip would probably be earning a well-deserved black eye. Let Maverick tweet about that.

Cecelia had done her part to put things right between them. The message was traveling through the interwebs, hopefully on its way to Deacon's inbox. She could already hear her cell phone buzzing in her purse, so the message was spreading at the speed of Royal gossip. Her father was probably having a heart attack on the imported living room rug at that exact moment, and her mother was calling to chastise and disown her. That was fine by her. She was more interested in being a Chase than a Morgan anyway.

If everyone else was seeing it, Deacon should, too. Surely when he read the message he could come out of hiding and seek her out. She couldn't very well locate him, if the last few days were any indication. No, she'd left a digital breadcrumb trail for Deacon to follow, and all she could do was to sit back, wait for the love of her life to sweep her off her feet and brace herself for her world to change forever.

Deacon was used to being invisible in Royal. As a kid, most people had paid him no mind, and not much had changed over the years, despite his

Cinderella moment at The Bellamy grand opening. He'd considered bailing on the town entirely after the fiasco with Chip, but something had kept him here. Whether it was his obligation to Shane or his misguided feelings for Cecelia, he wasn't sure. Either way, he knew he wasn't staying long, but in the meantime, the most effective course was for him to hide in plain sight—at The Bellamy itself.

He pulled the laptop out of his bag and set it up at the modern glass-and-chrome desk that was a feature of the penthouse suite. He could go downstairs to his office, but he ran the risk of running into someone and having to answer questions. Shane knew he was up here, but he had respected his space so far and promised he wouldn't reveal his whereabouts.

He'd never actually left the hotel that night. He'd marched through the bowels of the building trying to burn off his anger, then he'd had the front desk code him a key for the unoccupied penthouse suite, and he'd been there ever since. He'd left only to move his car from the employee lot to the virtually empty parking garage for guests.

He'd returned to the lobby just long enough to see Chip holding Cecelia's hand as they spoke to one another in a dark, quiet corridor near their offices. Hearing Chip boast had been bad enough, but it was like a knife to his gut to see them together like that.

He doubted anyone missed him, or was even looking for him, but if they were, they wouldn't expect him here. Why would he stay in a hotel with a perfectly lovely and secluded home only a few miles away?

To avoid Cecelia.

It was childish, he knew that. And perhaps she didn't give a damn where he was or what he was doing. She might be off making lavish wedding plans with Ashford for the social event of the year. If she *was* looking for him, it might just be to apologize for leading him on or to thank him for the lovely trip to France. Thanks, bye.

Either way, he didn't want to know what she had to say to him. He'd heard plenty that night from Chip. She'd made her decision, wrong as it might be, and he would live with it. He just didn't have to stick around so they could rub it in his face. He was going to make sure the hotel was running smoothly, hand over the reins to Shane, put his rustic lodge up for sale and return to his role as The Bellamy's silent, and invisible, partner.

Hell, if Shane could buy him out, he'd let him. Then he'd have no reason or need to ever set foot in the state of Texas again.

Maybe once he returned to Cannes, he could

wipe Chip's smug face from his memory. Deacon hadn't even known they were competing for the same woman until Chip announced that he had won. Of course he'd won. Chip didn't believe for a moment that Deacon was his competition. And despite the strides he'd made over the years, Deacon wasn't sure he was Ashford's competition, either.

They offered Cecelia different things. They both had money and good looks, so with that canceling out, Chip had things Deacon simply couldn't give her. Could never give her. Like a good family name, political connections and peace at home with her parents. That couldn't be bought, no matter how much money he made.

Then again, Chip didn't deserve a woman like Cecelia in his life. Not even with all that he could offer her, because he just wasn't a good person. He wasn't nice to Cecelia, much less to the little people whose votes he was constantly chasing. The only question was whether Cecelia knew that and appreciated what that meant for her future. If she even cared.

In France, away from her parents and the pressures of Royal, she had been free to be the person she wanted to be. That was the person he loved. But apparently those two Cecelias couldn't coexist back home. Within days of returning to Texas, she'd not only changed her mind about Deacon...

changed her mind about who she wanted to be and how she wanted to live…but she'd decided to take Chip back. Never mind how cruel he'd been, or how he'd kicked her when she was down. Once he was willing to "overlook" her shortcomings and take her back, she'd fallen into his arms.

Apparently she preferred being the good robot her parents wanted her to be than the happy, free spirit he saw inside her. And if that was the case, Deacon was fine moving on without her in his life. He didn't want *that* Cecelia anyway.

The suite doorbell rang, pulling Deacon from his thoughts. He didn't know who it could be. He hadn't ordered room service, and housekeeping had already visited for the day. With a frown, he got up and went to the door. Through the peephole, he spotted Shane. Reluctantly, he opened the door. If something was wrong at the hotel, he needed to man up and deal with it, not barricade himself in the penthouse, even if it meant he might see Cecelia downstairs. "Hey," he said casually, trying to act as though they didn't both know he was hiding up here after getting his heart trampled.

"Hey." Shane had a strange expression on his face. It was a weird mix of excitement and apprehension, which made Deacon even more curious about this unexpected visit. "Have you been online?" Shane asked.

Deacon took a step back to let his business partner into the suite. "No," he admitted. "I've done some work, read some emails, but I haven't really felt like seeing what the rest of the world was up to the last few days." He certainly didn't want to see a new engagement announcement for Cecelia and Chip, or run across any type of society buzz about their upcoming wedding being back on despite her tragic, secret past. He intended to be far, far away from Royal, Texas, by the time that event took place.

Shane charged in, nearly buzzing with nervous excitement. "So you really haven't seen it?"

Deacon closed the door, slightly irritated at the intrusion. "Seen what, Shane? I told you, I've been living in a cave for the last few days."

"Wow. I'm so glad I came up here, then. You need to see this." Shane turned his back on him without elaborating further, ratcheting Deacon's irritation up a notch, and walked over to the computer. He sat down at the desk, silently typing information into the web browser.

"Can't you just tell me?" Deacon asked as he came up behind him.

"No," Shane said. "You have to see this for yourself."

Deacon tried not to roll his eyes. He crossed his arms over his chest and waited impatiently for

Shane to pull up whatever important news had to be seen firsthand. At the moment, all he could see was that he'd pulled up Facebook. Deacon didn't even have a Facebook account. He didn't need a social site to remind him that he didn't really have any friends to keep up with online.

"Here," Shane said at last. He pointed to the screen as he got up from the chair. "Sit down and read this."

Deacon didn't argue. He sat down and looked at the post Shane had pointed out. It was a post from Cecelia's Facebook account. Her screen icon was a selfie that the two of them had taken when they were walking on the beach in Cannes. That was an odd choice for a woman who was engaged to another man, he thought. Then he read the words, and his heart stopped in his chest.

"Despite persistent rumors to the contrary, I am not, and never will be, engaged to Chip Ashford ever again. I would much rather be Mrs. Deacon Chase, and I hope that after everything that has happened between us, he will believe that and know how much I love him."

Deacon sat back against the plush leather of his computer chair and tried to absorb everything he'd read. She wasn't engaged to Chip? Had the smug bastard lied to Deacon's face about the whole thing? Was he so arrogant that he'd assumed she'd take him back if he only asked? That was a bold bluff, he had to give Chip that. From the sound of that post, it was a bluff that hadn't succeeded. If they really weren't together, that meant she still wanted to be with him.

Judging by her words, she wanted to be more than just with him. She wanted to spend the rest of her life with him.

She loved him.

It was a damn good thing Shane had made him sit down.

"Can you believe it?" Shane asked. "When I saw her that night at the party after you left, she seemed really confused by my congratulations on her engagement. I thought maybe she was just annoyed that the news got out before they could make an official announcement, but now it looks like it was because she didn't know what the hell I was talking about."

Deacon almost didn't believe what he was reading. He had been jerked around so many times where Cecelia was concerned that he was afraid to think it could really be true. He wanted it to be true, though. He'd made the mistake of letting himself fall in love with her again these past few weeks. He'd never intended on it, but after that afternoon in Provence, he couldn't help himself. He was madly in love with Cecelia Morgan. Could she really, truly be in love with him, as well?

"What are you going to do?" Shane pressed.

"I have no earthly idea," he answered. And that was the truth. He didn't want to screw this up. If he and Cecelia got back together, that was it. It was for life. He was going to marry her, make it official and never let that sweet creature out of his sight again. Even if that meant living in Royal for the rest of his life. It was the sacrifice he was willing to make to have her as his wife.

"Well, are you just going to sit here? Why aren't you rushing out the door to sweep her off her feet? She wants to marry you, Deacon. Stop hiding in this damn penthouse suite and do something about it."

Deacon closed his laptop screen and turned to face Shane. "I want to do this right. I can't half ass it on a whim. She deserves better than that. I don't think the little jewelry store in town is going to have what I need. Care to join me for a trip to Florida to get the perfect engagement ring?"

Shane grinned. "Florida? Just for a ring? There're some great places in Houston."

Deacon shook his head. "There's only one ring in the world for Cecelia, and it's in Florida."

"Okay," Shane agreed. "Do we need to have my assistant book some first-class tickets?"

"First class?" Deacon smirked, then shook his head as he reached for his phone. "Nope. We're taking a private jet."

Twelve

Cecelia slipped the key card into the elevator panel, allowing her to go to the restricted top floor of The Bellamy. When her message went out into the universe and everyone but Deacon seemed to receive it, she decided it was time to take some drastic measures. Someone had known where he was. Her money had been on Shane, but she'd opted to approach his fiancé instead. It was a risk, considering how Brandee probably felt about her, but she was her only hope. Brandee would likely have had the information without that pesky sense of loyalty to a friend.

It turned out she was right. Brandee not only gave her Deacon's location, but the access card to get her there. She had seen the posts online and, despite everything, was all too happy to help Cecelia reunite with Deacon.

The elevator chimed and the doors opened. Cecelia stepped out onto a small, elegant landing. There were doors at each end of the hallway. One was labeled the Lone Star Suite and the other the Rio Grande Suite. Brandee said that Deacon was in the former, so she took a deep breath to steel her courage and turned left toward his room and, hopefully, her future.

Facing the massive oak door, she raised her hand to knock but was surprised when the door whipped open before she could make contact.

Deacon was standing there, looking just as startled to find Cecelia on his doorstep. He was wearing an immaculately tailored dark gray suit with a sapphire-blue shirt that reminded her of the color of the ocean in Cannes. It clung to every angle and line of his body, making him look impossibly tall and more handsome than she could even remember.

Their sudden face-to-face stole the words from Cecelia's lips.

"Cecelia? What are you doing here?" he asked.

She bit anxiously at her lip. "Brandee told me where you were. I'm sorry, but I had to talk to you about something. It looks like you're headed out the door, though, so I guess I'll come back."

"No!" Deacon shouted, catching her upper arm before she could turn away to leave. "No, I was going to find you."

Cecelia felt a bit of the pressure crushing her rib cage lift. "You were?"

"Yes, please come in." Deacon stepped back and held out his arm for her to follow him into the suite.

She made her way into the room and over to the seating area with the modern couches she'd designed and had manufactured. It felt a little weird to be sitting on them as a guest. "You're a hard man to find," she admitted.

Deacon sat down on the sofa beside her, angling his shoulders and hips to face her. "I didn't want to be found. Especially by you."

The words were like a kick to her gut, but she had to understand where he was coming from. He didn't know the truth. "You know that Chip is a boastful liar, right? I hadn't seen or spoken to him since we broke up, and I certainly hadn't agreed to marry him before you two had your run-in at the party."

Deacon nodded. "I know. Shane showed me your post yesterday."

"Yesterday?" He'd seen it and done nothing. Why had he waited? She'd put her heart on the

line, and he'd sat back and thought about it over-
night. She'd been in misery, on pins and needles,
waiting to hear from him. That was the only reason she'd come after him. If he wasn't swayed by
her declaration of love and desire to marry, he at
least needed to know he was going to be a father.

"I had a lot to think about after I saw that."

"Well, I came here today because I have more
to say to you than can fit in one hundred and forty
characters. I also need to say things that don't need
to be posted for the whole world to read. Not because I'm ashamed of them or you, but because
some things are meant to be private, and between
two people."

She closed her eyes for a moment to gather her
thoughts. She had a lot to say, and she wanted to say
it just right. "First, I wanted to thank you."

"Thank me?" Deacon looked surprised.

"Yes. You've taught me how to feel again. To
love again. After we broke up, it hurt so badly to
lose you that I shut down inside. I couldn't bear the
pain, and I didn't want to fall in love with someone
else and lose them, too. I decided I was done with
love and I was going to focus on my career instead.
I built baby furniture because a part of me thought
it would be as close as I would ever get to having children. At least with a loving partner. I con-

vinced myself that a loveless marriage that made good business sense was the right choice.

"I was wrong about everything. I didn't know I was starving until you gave me a taste of what I'd been missing. Then I knew I was wrong to close off my heart, wrong to think Chip was the kind of person I needed in my life... But most of all, I was wrong to think that I could ever stop loving you, no matter how hard I tried to suppress it."

She hesitated for a moment and turned to look at him so he would be able to sense and feel how much she meant the words she was about to say. "You are the only person I've ever known who loved me just the way I was. No restrictions, no requirements. So I wanted to thank you for that."

Deacon stared at her silently for a moment, and then he reached out to take Cecelia's hand in his own. "I've never stopped loving you, Cecelia. Even when I was angry or hurt, I still loved you. You're the reason I haven't left Royal yet. There was no reason to stay, but a part of me just couldn't leave you behind, even if you'd chosen that greasy politician over me."

"I would never do that. He doesn't hold a candle to you. I don't understand why my parents can't see what kind of man he really is, but in the end it doesn't matter. In France, I decided I was going to live my own life on my own terms, and that hasn't changed. If my parents come around, they can be in my life, but if they don't, I'm okay with that. I'm never choosing them over you again."

Deacon squeezed her hand as she spoke. "You have no idea how happy I am to hear you say that. I've got a few things I need to tell you, as well."

"I wasn't finished," Cecelia said, but he raised his hand to shush her. She hadn't gotten to the critical news yet.

"I've been doing a lot of thinking while I've been holed up in his hotel suite. Your message and your arrival here today made things easier, but I was determined to change things between us before that happened. I walked away that night when I was faced with Chip's challenge, and I shouldn't have. Suddenly, I was eighteen again and not good enough for you. I walked away that night all those years ago, and I walked away again, instead of fighting for your love the way I should have. I'm not making that mistake again because you are worth fighting for.

"When I ran into you at the door just now, I was coming to tell you how much I loved you. Even if Chip had convinced you to take him back, I was going to steal you away, and I knew I could because he could never give you what you really needed. I'm the only one who can love you the way you need to be loved. I want to give you that life you've dreamed of, the family you've always wanted. I am determined to give you everything your heart desires. Starting with this."

Deacon reached into his coat pocket and pulled out a black velvet box. "I was on my way to find you and give you this. You said you wanted to be Mrs. Deacon Chase, and I didn't want to make you wait a moment longer. I didn't immediately come running to you because I wanted to have the right ring, the right words, the right suit… I wanted this moment to be perfect."

Cecelia shook her head with tears glistening in her eyes. "It is perfect, Deacon. You could be in jeans with a grape ring pop and I would say yes because you're the best thing that's ever happened to me."

Deacon smiled. "This is a little better than a grape ring pop."

He opened the box, revealing the prettiest vintage ring she'd ever seen. It had a round diamond set in a thin rose-gold band. A circle of small diamonds set in rose gold surrounded the center stone, and intricate scrolls were cut into the setting and along the sides. Cecelia had never seen anything like it.

"I didn't want to compete with Chip to get you the biggest, gaudiest diamond I could. Instead, I wanted to get you the most meaningful ring I could.

This one belonged to my grandmother. Shane and I flew to Florida yesterday to get it from my parents."

Deacon plucked the ring from its velvet bed and held it up to her. "Cecelia, this question has been a long time coming, but will you be my wife?"

Cecelia had been asked that question one time before, but this was completely different. There were butterflies in her stomach, her heart was racing and she couldn't take her eyes off the beautiful ring. When Chip proposed, she didn't know what it should feel like. Accepting his proposal had been like signing the paperwork to buy a new car—nice and satisfying, but not exactly a moment to cherish for a lifetime. This blew everything out of the water.

"Yes!" she said, bubbling over with love and enthusiasm. "I've been waiting to be Mrs. Deacon Chase since I was seventeen years old."

Deacon slipped the ring on her finger. It fit perfectly. The minute he read the message from Cecelia online, he knew this was the ring for her. His grandmother had told him as a child that her ring was to be kept so he could give it to the love of his life one day. Her marriage had been full of love and laughter, and she wanted the same for him. Even in their hardest financial times, his parents refused to sell the ring. He would need it one day, they insisted.

And based on the light in her eyes and the smile on her face, she liked it. The anxious muscles in his neck and shoulders started to relax now that she'd said yes. He snaked his arms around Cecelia's waist and tugged her to him. Their lips met, and suddenly it felt as though all was right with the world. Cecelia was going to be his wife. Nothing else mattered.

When their lips finally parted, Deacon studied Cecelia's face for a moment. "You've been waiting a while to be married to me. How much longer do you want to wait to make it official? We can be on a jet to Las Vegas in an hour."

Her nose wrinkled as she considered his offer. The idea of her being his wife before the sun went down was intriguing. Their relationship had come apart so many times, he was keen to make it legal once and for all before she could slip through his fingers again.

"No," she said at last. "I want to be your wife more than anything, but I don't want to elope. I want this whole town to put on their best cowboy boots, go down to the church and witness you and me making vows to love one another until the end of time. I want my parents to see it. The Ashfords to see it. I even hope Maverick will be sitting in those pews, so he'll know that he didn't win this time, not with me."

Deacon couldn't have been more proud of his fiancée than he was in that moment. Even if he had come to terms with this town and what people thought of him, it made him happy to see that she was proud to be his wife. "They'd better get used to having me around anyway."

Cecelia perked up beside him. "Does that mean you're willing to move here?"

He hadn't given it a lot of thought, but yes, if that was what she wanted. "I'd live on the moon if that's where you were. I'll have to travel quite a bit to my various hotels, but if you want Royal to be home, that's fine with me."

"Can we spend the summers in France?"

Deacon grinned. "You bet. I can't say no to you. If you want to live here, we'll live here. If you want a big church wedding with four hundred guests, let's do it. I happen to know the guy who owns the big new hotel in town, if you want to have a reception there. Anything you want, you'll have it. The white dress, the church, the flowers, the whole thing. Go buck wild, baby."

"I won't go too crazy," she said, although he could already see the wheels turning in her head with wedding plans. "I still want to marry you as soon as possible. Maybe not tonight, but soon."

That was fine by him. All he wanted was to be married. Cake, flowers and all the other trappings of the ceremony were unnecessary distractions to him, but he understood their importance to her. "Okay. We'll get the engagement announcement in the Sunday paper. Or shall we go post the good news online before Maverick can beat us to the punch?" Deacon asked in a joking tone.

Cecelia shook her head. "Not yet. I want to keep this just between us for a day or two. And besides that, Maverick doesn't know everything. I've got another little secret of my own."

Deacon's brow raised in curiosity. What other big news could she possibly have to share? "What's that?"

She untangled her fingers from his and placed his hand across her stomach. "I'm having Deacon Chase's baby."

Deacon didn't think that he could be stunned speechless, but she'd just done it. His baby? She was pregnant with his baby? He looked down at his hand and the still-flat belly beneath it. "You're pregnant?"

"Yes. You're happy, aren't you? Please say you're happy."

He pinned her with his gaze so there were no doubts in her mind about how he felt. "I'm thrilled beyond belief. I'm just not sure how it happened.

We were careful, weren't we? How far along are you?"

"Four weeks. I think it happened that first night we were together, when I threw myself at you."

Deacon arched an eyebrow. "The day you sneaked out on me?"

"Yes," she admitted with a sheepish grin. "I guess I would've been back no matter what."

Deacon couldn't even imagine how he would've taken the news if she had shown up after her disappearing act and announced she was having his baby. He was nearly blown off his feet as it was. "How long have you known?" he asked.

"I started feeling poorly on the flight back from Cannes. I thought I was just airsick, but when it persisted a few days, I realized there might be more to it. I bought a pregnancy test the night of The Bellamy's grand opening. That's why I was late to the party. When I did arrive, I was looking all over for you to tell you the news, but you'd already left after arguing with Chip. When I realized what had happened, I was heartbroken, but I couldn't find you to tell you the truth."

Deacon squeezed his eyes shut to keep from getting angry. Not at her, but with himself. He'd ruined that moment they would've shared together because he thought so little of himself that he let Chip scare him off. There she'd been, searching the crowd to tell him they were having a baby, and he was lick-. ing his wounds in the penthouse.

"I am so sorry," he said. "I let Chip ruin that night for us. We should've spent this week together picking out baby names and planning our future together."

"I don't care about that," Cecelia insisted. "It's just a few days in the scheme of things, and it gave us both some time to figure out what we really wanted, baby or no baby. What matters is that you and I love each other, we're getting married and we're having a baby. I've always wanted a family of my own, and now I'm going to have it. With you."

Deacon pulled Cecelia close again, this time tugging her all the way into his lap. He cradled her in his arms, capturing her lips in the kind of kiss he'd fantasized about since they got back to Texas. She melted into him, reminding him just how much he'd missed her touch these last few days.

"If you're having my baby, maybe we should reconsider the Vegas option and get married tonight."

Cecelia shook her head. "This isn't a shotgun wedding, Deacon, and I don't want anyone to think so. Besides, I think a baby is the perfect wedding gift, don't you?"

It sounded good to him. "If that's what you want, I'm glad to be the one to give it to you."

Cecelia laid her head on his shoulder and sighed

contentedly. Deacon could feel her warm breath against his skin, and it sent a shiver through his body. He was tired of talking about plans and exes and blackmailers. He wanted to lay claim to the mother of his child. He stood without warning, making Cecelia squeal and cling to his neck.

"What are you doing?" she asked.

"I'm making good use of the king-size bed in the penthouse suite to make love to my fiancée."

She didn't complain. She just held on until he placed her gently on the bed. "After everything that's happened, do you think everyone will be surprised to find out that you've won me back?"

Deacon hovered over her and planted a soft kiss on her lips. His fingers sought out the buttons of her blouse and started working them open. He slipped one hand inside to cup her breast through the lacy fabric she liked. She gasped, arching up off the bed.

"I didn't win you back, Cecelia. You've always been mine."

* * * * *

Don't miss a single installment of the
TEXAS CATTLEMAN'S CLUB: BLACKMAIL
No secret—or heart—is safe in Royal, Texas...

THE TYCOON'S SECRET CHILD by
USA TODAY *bestselling author Maureen Child*

TWO-WEEK TEXAS SEDUCTION by
Cat Schield

REUNITED WITH THE RANCHER by
USA TODAY *bestselling author Sara Orwig*

EXPECTING THE BILLIONAIRE'S BABY by
Andrea Laurence

and

May 2017: TRIPLETS FOR THE TEXAN by
USA TODAY *bestselling author Janice Maynard*

June 2017: A TEXAS-SIZED SECRET by
USA TODAY *bestselling author Maureen Child*

COMING NEXT MONTH FROM

HARLEQUIN *Desire*

Available May 9, 2017

#2515 THE MARRIAGE CONTRACT
Billionaires and Babies • by Kat Cantrell

Longing for a child of his own, reclusive billionaire Des marries McKenna in name only so she can bear his child, but when complications force them to live as man and wife, the temptation is to make the marriage real...

#2516 TRIPLETS FOR THE TEXAN
Texas Cattleman's Club: Blackmail • by Janice Maynard

Wealthy Texas doctor Troy "Hutch" Hutchinson is the one who got away. Now he's back and ready to make things right, but Simone is already expecting three little surprises of her own...

#2517 LITTLE SECRET, RED HOT SCANDAL
Las Vegas Nights • by Cat Schield

Superstar Nate Tucker has no interest in the spoiled pop princess determined to ensnare him, but when a secret affair with her quiet sister, Mia, results in a baby on the way, he'll do whatever it takes to claim Mia as his.

#2518 THE RANCHER'S CINDERELLA BRIDE
Callahan's Clan • by Sara Orwig

When Gabe agrees to a fake engagement with his best friend, Meg, he doesn't expect to fight temptation at every turn. But a makeover leads to the wildest kiss of his life and now he wants to find out if friends make the best lovers...

#2519 THE MAGNATE'S MARRIAGE MERGER
The McNeill Magnates • by Joanne Rock

Matchmaker Lydia Whitney has been secretly exacting revenge on her wealthy ex-lover, but when he discovers her true identity, it's his turn to exact the sweetest revenge...by making her his convenient wife!

#2520 TYCOON COWBOY'S BABY SURPRISE
The Wild Caruthers Bachelors • by Katherine Garbera

What happens in Vegas should stay there, but when Kinley Quinten shows up in Cole's Hill, Texas, to plan a wedding, the groom's very familiar brother's attempts to rekindle their fling is hindered by a little secret she kept years ago...

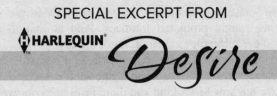
*Superstar Nate Tucker has no interest in the spoiled pop
princess determined to ensnare him, but when a secret
affair with her quiet sister, Mia, results in a baby on the
way, he'll do whatever it takes to claim Mia as his.*

Read on for a sneak peek at
LITTLE SECRET, RED HOT SCANDAL
by Cat Schield

Mia had made her choice and it hadn't been him.

"How've you been?" He searched her face for some
sign she'd suffered as he had, lingering over the circles
under her eyes and the downward turn to her mouth. To
his relief she didn't look happy, but that didn't stop her
from putting on a show.

"Things have been great."

"Tell me the truth." He was asking after her welfare,
but what he really wanted to know was if she'd missed
him.

"I'm great. Really."

"I hope your sister gave you a little time off."

"Ivy was invited to a charity event in South Beach and
we extended our stay a couple days to kick back and soak
up some sun."

Ivy demanded all Mia's time and energy. That Nate
had spent any alone time with Mia during Ivy's eight-
week stint on his tour was nothing short of amazing.

They'd snuck around like teenage kids. The danger of getting caught promoted intimacy. And at first, Nate found the subterfuge amusing. It got old fast.

It had bothered Nate that Ivy treated Mia like an employee instead of a sister. She never seemed to appreciate how Mia's kind and thoughtful behavior went above and beyond the role of personal assistant.

"I don't like the way we left things between us," Nate declared, taking a step in her direction.

Mia took a matching step backward. "You asked for something I couldn't give you."

"I asked for you to come to Las Vegas with me."

"We'd barely known each other two months." It was the same excuse she'd given him three weeks ago and it rang as hollow now as it had then. "And I couldn't leave Ivy."

"She could've found another assistant." He'd said the same thing the morning after the tour ended. The night after Mia had stayed with him until the sun crested the horizon.

"I'm not just her assistant. I'm her sister," Mia said, now as then. "She needs me."

I need you.

He wouldn't repeat the words. It wouldn't do any good. She'd still choose obligation to her sister over being happy with him.

And he couldn't figure out why.

HARLEQUIN Desire

AVAILABLE MAY 2017

TRIPLETS FOR THE TEXAN

BY *USA TODAY* BESTSELLING AUTHOR

JANICE MAYNARD,

PART OF THE SIZZLING
TEXAS CATTLEMAN'S CLUB: BLACKMAIL SERIES.

Wealthy Texas doctor Troy "Hutch" Hutchinson is the one who got away. Now he's back and ready to make things right, but Simone is already expecting three little surprises of her own...

AND DON'T MISS A SINGLE INSTALLMENT OF

BLACKMAIL

No secret—or heart—is safe in Royal, Texas...

The Tycoon's Secret Child
by *USA TODAY* bestselling author Maureen Child

Two-Week Texas Seduction by Cat Schield

Reunited with the Rancher
by *USA TODAY* bestselling author Sara Orwig

Expecting the Billionaire's Baby by Andrea Laurence

Triplets for the Texan
by *USA TODAY* bestselling author Janice Maynard

AND

June 2017: *A Texas-Sized Secret* by *USA TODAY* bestselling author Maureen Child
July 2017: *Lone Star Baby Scandal* by Golden Heart® Award winner Lauren Canan
August 2017: *Tempted by the Wrong Twin* by *USA TODAY* bestselling author Rachel Bailey
September 2017: *Taking Home the Tycoon* by *USA TODAY* bestselling author Catherine Mann
October 2017: *Billionaire's Baby Bind* by *USA TODAY* bestselling author Katherine Garbera
November 2017: *The Texan Takes a Wife* by *USA TODAY* bestselling author Charlene Sands
December 2017: *Best Man Under the Mistletoe* by *USA TODAY* bestselling author Kathie DeNosky

Whatever You're Into… Passionate Reads

Looking for more passionate reads from Harlequin®?
Fear not! Harlequin® Presents, Harlequin® Desire and
Harlequin® Blaze offer you irresistible romance stories
featuring powerful heroes.

⬥HARLEQUIN *Presents.*

Do you want alpha males, decadent glamour and jet-set
lifestyles? Step into the sensational, sophisticated world of
Harlequin® Presents, where sinfully tempting heroes ignite a
fierce and wickedly irresistible passion!

⬥HARLEQUIN *Desire*

Harlequin® Desire novels are powerful, passionate and
provocative contemporary romances set against a backdrop of
wealth, privilege and sweeping family saga. Alpha heroes with
a soft side meet strong-willed but vulnerable heroines amid a
dramatic world of divided loyalties, high-stakes conflict and
intense emotion.

⬥HARLEQUIN *Blaze*

Harlequin® Blaze stories sizzle with strong heroines and
irresistible heroes playing the game of modern love and lust.
They're fun, sexy and always steamy.

Be sure to check out our full selection of books
within each series every month!

www.Harlequin.com

Get 2 Free Books,
Plus 2 Free Gifts—
just for trying the Reader Service!

⬦HARLEQUIN *Desire*